"I'll come."

Did her voice just tremble? "Thanksgiving," she clarified. "Thank you for the invite." She turned to go upstairs before she made a fool of herself when the tears came.

"You're going to cry," he said softly and there was an undertone of horror that would have made her laugh under different circumstances.

Josh couldn't help it. Those big blue eyes shimmering with tears simply did him in. He touched her face, the warm satin of her skin. Smelled the fresh, fruity scent of shampoo from her still-damp hair. Heard her sharp intake of breath as her hand came up to rest on his chest, but she didn't pull away. His gaze locked on her blue one, and he saw his own desire reflected in hers. The wanting twined around them, silky, sweet and hot.

Dangerous.

THE NANNY'S CHRISTMAS WISH

BY
AMI WEAVER

MILLS & BOON

First published in Great Britain 2013
by Mills & Boon, an imprint of Harlequin (UK) Limited,
Eton House, 18-24 Paradise Road, Richmond, Surrey TW9 1SR

© Ami Weaver 2013

ISBN: 978 0 263 90161 0

23-1113

Harlequin (UK) policy is to use papers that are natural, renewable and recyclable products and made from wood grown in sustainable forests. The logging and manufacturing processes conform to the legal environmental regulations of the country of origin.

Printed and bound in Spain
by Blackprint CPI, Barcelona

Two-time Golden Heart® Award finalist **Ami Weaver** has been reading romance since she was a teen and writing for even longer, so it was only natural she would put the two together. Now she can be found drinking gallons of iced tea at her local coffee shop while doing one of her very favorite things—convincing two characters they deserve their happy-ever-after. When she's not writing, she enjoys time spent at the lake, hanging out with her family and reading. Ami lives in Michigan with her four kids, three cats and her very supportive husband.

For Stacy, my long-ago writing partner—
so you won't forget our early stories.
Thanks for being a good friend for so many years.

Chapter One

Thirty-Eight Easton Street. Maggie Thelan double-checked the address on the big blue Victorian with the sticky note on the steering wheel. Her pulse kicked up a bit as she eased the car to the curb.

She drew in a deep breath and let it out slowly, trying to calm the butterflies in her belly. Cody, her nephew, lived here. Her half sister, Lucy, had lived here until her death. It would be Maggie's home during her stint as Cody's nanny.

If she got the job.

No way am I missing this chance. She grabbed her purse and keys and checked her reflection in the rearview mirror. Hair behaving, mascara not smeared, all good. She did a quick application of lip gloss and wondered for the millionth time if she shared her Black Irish coloring—dark hair, blue eyes, pale skin—with her half sister.

With any luck there'd be a photo out for Maggie to see. Anticipation quivered through her as she threw open the car door.

She'd gotten through the first interview just fine. Cody's grandmother, Ellen Tanner, was a lovely woman, warm and friendly and concerned about her grandson's welfare. This time, she'd meet Cody and his father and hopefully walk away with the job.

She'd staked everything on it.

Not wanting to think about that, Maggie hurried up the

walk, her ponytail blowing over her shoulder in the wind. Being October in northern Michigan, the breeze had a bite to it but the sun still held some warmth. The maple trees on the front lawn blazed gold and flame.

A couple of squat pumpkins sat on the front porch. Maggie stepped around them and up to the heavy front door.

She pressed the doorbell and the door opened almost instantly, causing her to take a big step back and stumble over one of the pumpkins behind her. "Whoa," said a deep voice, and he grabbed her elbow before she ended up smashing the pumpkin under her rear. She pitched forward and felt a firm, broad chest under her cheek. He smelled of clean laundry and soap. Warmth seeped through his blue oxford dress shirt.

Or maybe that was her face, burning with embarrassment.

Smooth, Maggie, real smooth. She stepped back, carefully this time, cleared her throat and promptly forgot what she'd been about to say as her gaze traveled up.

Oh, he was tall, north of six feet and broad, with light brown hair that curled slightly at the nape. And his eyes. Damn if she hadn't just lost her voice in those whiskey-colored eyes.

"You all right?" His voice, laced with amusement and concern, snapped Maggie out of her trance.

"Yes. Thanks for the help." She thrust out her hand as she tried to recover her scattered wits. "Maggie Thelan. I'm here for a second interview for the nanny position."

He raised his eyebrows, arched over those incredible eyes. They weren't the color of just any whiskey, but the good Scotch stuff her father had favored. Her heart pinged. The man grasped her hand, his palm warm and slightly rough on hers. She sucked in a breath at the unwelcome little shiver that zipped up her arm. "Dr. Josh Tanner. Nice to meet you," he said as he released his grip.

"You, too," she replied. Dread seized her. This man was Cody's dad. What if he thought she'd be a klutzy danger to his son? *Good one, Maggie.*

He stepped back. "Come on in. Have a seat over there." He indicated the sofa in a comfortable living room. *Photos.* Her pulse picked up a bit as she made her way to sit down.

She cleared her throat and smiled as he sat down opposite her. She peeked around him at the pictures on the mantel. *Shoot.* Some of them were too small to see the subjects clearly. She snapped her focus back to find him studying her with a crease between his eyebrows.

Her stomach clenched. "Is there a problem?"

He hesitated a spilt second. "I have to say I was expecting someone older. I told my mom—" He broke off and the frown deepened.

"What?" Her stomach tightened. "Why do you need someone older?"

"I just thought, well, more experience, maybe." He had the grace to look slightly embarrassed.

Maggie's eyebrows shot up and she straightened her spine, spearing him with the look that had sent plenty of fourth-graders scurrying back in line. "I've been a teacher for ten years, Dr. Tanner. I assure you, I have plenty of experience with kids."

He nodded, reluctance still etched on his face. "I saw that on your résumé. You are by far the most highly qualified candidate. My mom thinks highly of you and I trust her judgment. Your background check is clean and the references are excellent, so as long as Cody likes you we'll consider this a done deal."

Relief flooded Maggie even as she noted he didn't look pleased about the whole thing. "Thank you. I hope he does,

Doctor. I'm looking forward to meeting him." *More than you'll ever know.* The chance to know Cody, hopefully learn something about her half sister, meant everything to her. Her heart squeezed. Since her father's death and learning he had kept his older daughter a secret, Maggie's world had been in a tailspin.

He glanced at his watch. "While we're waiting, do you want to see where you'll be staying?" he asked.

"I'd love to," she said.

A quick perusal of the mantel on her way past revealed photos of Cody, either alone or with his dad or Grandma. Nothing of Lucy. She climbed the creaking stairs behind Dr. Tanner and since it felt wrong to look at the view of his rear she kept her eyes at his waist. His pants were frayed at the belt loops, a little detail at odds with the crisp pleats in the front.

Upstairs, he walked past three rooms to the end of the hall and pushed open a door. "This be okay for you?"

Maggie stepped around him, catching a whiff of his scent as she did so. The little jolt of awareness was almost drowned out by the pleasure that flooded her at the room.

"This is beautiful!"

The room was huge and she could see a balcony through French doors. A four-poster bed sat across from the fire-place, where a cozy little grouping of furniture had been arranged. She could picture herself reading to Cody there, snuggling by the fire on a cold and snowy night.

A little shiver of joy ran through her. She couldn't ask for a more perfect setting to get to know her nephew.

"There are plenty of extra sheets if you want to use them, and comforters, too. Not sure what you'd like, but if you don't find something that works just buy what you want and I'll cover it. Bathroom's in here." Dr. Tanner stepped around her and pointed to the first of two doors. "Closet's the next one."

Maggie pulled open the door and peeked in at the bathroom. Double sinks, oversize tub, separate shower. Fresh towels, no doubt his mother's touch, on the towel rack.

A master bedroom. Why didn't he use the master? Too many memories?

"Dr. Tanner, really, this is amazing. I love it." She moved over the plush carpeting to the four-poster and ran her hand over the smooth wood of the footboard. Unless she missed her guess, this bed was an antique.

When she looked up, she caught him watching her with caution and something else, a something that made her skin get hot and reminded her she was alone with a gorgeous man. In a room with a bed.

The one man she couldn't have and wouldn't want anyway.

So why had her mouth just gone dry?

"Josh," he said, and Maggie blinked, her thoughts thankfully derailed. "Call me Josh, please. You're not my patient."

"Josh, then," she murmured.

A banging from downstairs made them both jump, shattering the awkward moment.

"That'd be Cody and my mother," he said, relief clear in his voice. "Let's go meet them."

Cody Tanner, age four, looked up at Maggie with serious blue eyes ringed with long, dark lashes. Light brown curls haloed around his head. Her heart melted, and emotion crashed over her in a fierce wave. She ached to pull him in her arms. This little boy was the only link to the half sister she'd never have the chance to know. He dropped his gaze to her feet and she swallowed hard.

"Hi, Cody." Maggie stuck out her hand, but Cody ignored it, instead pressing against his grandmother's leg. She tried to ignore the sharp sting his rejection produced.

"Code," his father said in a gentle voice, "you can do better than that."

Cody looked up at Maggie, his big blue eyes swimming with tears, and shook his head.

Maggie's heart cracked. "It's okay—" she began but Josh shook his head.

"Cody, we talked about this. Remember?"

"Don't want her," Cody cried and Maggie sucked in her breath, each word almost a physical blow. "I wanna have Mrs. Herman!"

Josh knelt down in front of his son. He tugged Cody into his arms. "I know it's hard on you. But she had to leave, Code," he said. "You know that. She had to go help her daughter out. She'll miss you and she loves you. She'll call and send you letters. Remember?"

Cody dipped his chin. "I know," he mumbled, and his father hugged him.

"Now, let's try this again. What do you say to Ms. Thelan?"

Cody slid a sideways glance her way. "Hi," he muttered and Maggie smiled.

"Nice to meet you, Cody." Oh, if he only knew.

Ellen held out her hand to her grandson. "Cody, you want to help me make some sandwiches for lunch?"

Cody brightened. "C'n I have peanut butter?"

"Of course. You can even spread the jelly if you want."

"Okay." With a last cautious glance at Maggie, Cody followed Ellen into the kitchen.

Josh looked at Maggie. "Mrs. Herman is Cody's former nanny. Her leaving has been hard on him. I'm sorry you had to see that."

"Don't be," Maggie said, and meant it. "He is attached to Mrs. Herman. It's a loss he has to process. I understand. It'll take some time, but we'll be okay."

Maggie held her breath while Josh gave her a thoughtful look. "Let's have a seat and go over what exactly you'll be doing."

Maggie's heart soared. "Does this mean I officially have the job?"

"Yes."

Even with the reluctance in his voice, relief flooded her. Maybe her luck had finally turned, after all.

Too young.

Later that evening, Josh's thought upon seeing Maggie Thelan for the first time kept playing through his head. And too gorgeous, with that long dark hair and those blue, blue eyes rimmed with dark lashes. Similar to Lucy's, really, but hers had been a paler blue. He pulled his thoughts back to the problem at hand.

His mother was playing matchmaker.

He groaned and clicked the TV remote, not seeing the images on the screen. He'd specifically requested an older woman so there'd be no chance of anyone thinking there was anything remotely marriageable about him. That possibility died with Lucy, as it should have.

But Mom clearly had other plans. She'd told him over and over to move on. To let Lucy go. He'd listened politely, but he knew it didn't matter. He'd made a promise to her, intended to keep it. He'd managed it for nearly four years.

But then Maggie stumbled into his life and now things were not quite so cut and dried. She made something he'd buried long ago want to sit up and take notice.

Josh groaned again and scrubbed his hand over his eyes.

Hell. She'd be the nanny. Meaning she'd be living here, under his roof, right down the hall from his bedroom.

Josh shifted on the bed. Uh-uh. No way could his thoughts take that course. No.

Maybe he could tell her he'd changed his mind, they didn't need her and he'd go find a nanny on his own.

A nice, grandmotherly type. Someone who wouldn't remind him he couldn't get involved with another woman.

"Daddy?" Cody's voice sliced across his thoughts.

"Cody. I thought you were sleeping." Josh hit the mute button on the TV. He patted the bed beside him. "You okay?"

Cody nodded as he crawled up next to Josh. "Yeah. Is Miz Thelan gonna be my new nanny?" His voice dropped off.

"Mrs. Herman isn't coming back," Josh said gently. "You know that, Code. We need someone to help us out around here. Ms. Thelan seems really nice. I think she'll be a good nanny."

So much for not hiring her.

Cody bit his lower lip. "But—don't—if I don't get a nanny won't Miz Herman hafta come back?" The words tumbled out in a rush.

"No. Oh, Cody, is that what you thought?" Josh's heart broke and he reached over to hug his son to his side, felt the little body nestle into his own.

Cody shrugged his small shoulders, then nodded.

Josh spoke gently, knowing how hard this had been for his son. "Cody, she loves you, but she had to go."

"Like Mama," Cody said matter-of-factly, and pain seared through Josh, cutting off his air for a heartbeat. *Like Mama.*

"Mama can't come back. But she loved you, too, Cody." His voice grated in his throat. Lucy had adored Cody, doted on him, loved him with every last fiber of her being. This Josh knew without a doubt. Guilt crushed him every time he thought of it. He was the reason his son didn't have a mother anymore.

"Miz Thelan is pretty," Cody said. Josh said nothing, stymied by the realization that he couldn't deny he agreed, or what it meant. "Will she live here? With you an' me, Daddy?"

"Yeah," Josh said and wondered again if having Maggie under his roof was a good plan.

"Then I guess it's okay to try her, Daddy." Cody's small face was serious. Josh hid a smile.

"Then we will. I think she'll be just fine."

"Is she gonna cook for us?"

Josh shrugged. "She said she could but we'll see."

They looked at each other for a moment, and Josh knew they were both thinking of Mrs. Herman's practical casseroles.

Years of casseroles.

"No, um, cassy-oles?" Cody ventured and Josh laughed.

"She doesn't look like the casserole type but we'll ask her tomorrow when she gets here just to be sure. Okay? Now let's get you back to bed."

"Okay." Cody slid off Josh's bed. Josh followed him across the hall and tucked Cody back in. He ran a hand over the boy's curls and Cody gave him a sleepy smile.

"G'night, Daddy."

"'Night, Code." Josh lingered for a moment, enjoying the little rustles Cody made as he settled. Then he returned to his room, flopped on the bed and stared at the ceiling.

Sleep wouldn't come easy for him tonight.

Maggie pulled in the driveway of the big blue house, her car packed to the gills. Everything else had gone into storage when she sublet her apartment. That had been a bit of a risk. If this nanny position had fallen through, she'd have been up you-know-what creek without a paddle.

At least it would be familiar territory.

She got out of the car and hesitated in the driveway. Hired or not, it didn't seem right to just walk in the house. Ellen burst out the front door.

"Maggie! Oh, my goodness, let me help. Josh, come on," she yelled over her shoulder. "Maggie's here." She hurried across the lawn and gave Maggie a quick hug. "Let Josh and me help you. Is this all you brought?" she asked as she opened a rear door.

"All?" Maggie laughed. The car practically groaned under the weight of her "necessities." The front door banged shut before she could say anything else and she turned to see Josh step out on the porch. His flannel shirt looked soft and worn with age, and his jeans held the same patina. His whiskey gaze caught hers and her traitorous pulse tripped. He gave her a half smile, strode down the steps.

"Good morning, Ms. Thelan," he said, his deep voice resonating in the very core of her.

"It's Maggie," she said, and mentally winced at the husky element in her voice.

"Maggie, then," he said and looked at her with… Was that regret?

"Josh! This box has books. Can you get it?" Ellen's voice reached them, and he turned toward his mother.

"Sure, Mom," he said. Maggie went around to the other side of the car as her insides twisted. Was Josh having second thoughts about hiring her? He'd been ambivalent, she knew, but she'd hoped a few days of space would have erased his doubts.

An hour later, she decided she'd imagined the whole

thing. Josh was polite, and said no more than necessary, but she didn't catch any more weird vibes from him. Ellen made up for it with chatter and Maggie was grateful for her warmth. Cody hovered around the edges of the activity, helping sometimes without being asked, but mostly dogging his father's shadow. Her heart ached for the boy.

She hoped by Monday he'd have accepted her enough that they could spend the day together comfortably.

"Okay," Ellen announced, placing a box on the floor by the bed. "Josh has the last one, he's coming up behind me. Looks like you've made progress already," she added, nodding to the closet where some clothes hung.

Maggie laughed. "That's why I leave all that stuff on hangers. Makes me feel like I've done a lot when actually... well, actually, I haven't." She sank down in a chair near the fireplace, looked around at the mess. "I can't thank you enough for helping me."

Ellen waved her hand, dismissing Maggie's thanks. "It was nothing, honey, really. Do you need any help unpacking?"

Maggie shook her head. She wouldn't ask for anything more even if she needed it. "No. Thanks, though. I'll be fine."

"Okay, then." Ellen crossed to the door, then stopped. "You have my number if you need it on Monday? If you have any questions at all, you can call. Josh can't always get away, but I'm usually available."

"I do have it. I'm sure we'll be fine, but it's a big comfort to know you're there if we get stuck," Maggie assured her. Ellen nodded.

"Okay, then. Sorry to run, but I'm meeting a friend for dinner and it's a good hour drive." She left, and Maggie heard her voice in the hall before Josh came in, carrying the last of the boxes.

"Where can I put this?" he asked.

She waved her hand. "Anywhere's fine. I have to go through them all anyway."

Josh deposited the box near the one his mother left and stood still. An awkward silence fell over the room as Maggie tried her hardest to look everywhere but at him, but her gaze kept darting back as if he were magnetic.

"I—"

"Do—"

They both stopped, and he dipped his head in her direction. "You first."

She drew in a deep breath. "I was just going to thank you for the help," she said. "It wasn't necessary but I really appreciate it."

"No problem. Do you like pizza? You're welcome to eat dinner with us."

Maggie hesitated. She needed to erect some kind of wall between her unexpected emotions and this man. On the other hand, it would be an opportunity to interact with Cody. "Will Cody mind if I join you? I don't want to infringe on his time with you."

Josh shook his head. "You won't be. It'll be good for you to spend some time together. Any requests for toppings? Anything you can't stand?"

They settled the pizza question with no onions or peppers for her but anything else was fair game. Josh left the room, pulling the door closed behind him. Maggie stared at the closed door, then flopped back on the bed as the enormity of her situation began to take root.

She'd found Cody, gotten the job she wanted so badly.

But she'd never figured on her brother-in-law. She hadn't counted on seeing him as an attractive man. Somehow, she needed to figure out how to ignore that while keeping her true relationship to Cody a secret from his father. A flash of guilt made her swallow hard. Would it have been better to own up to her connection to Lucy?

No. She stood up and moved to the nearest box. The last thing she wanted was to inflict any more pain on either Josh or Cody. They'd experienced a terrible loss before Cody's first birthday and she had no desire to open any old wounds for them. With any luck she could spend a year or so with Cody, and have enough of a relationship with the little boy that Josh would allow her to stay in his life after Cody no longer needed a nanny.

So she'd get over this ridiculous quasi-attraction to Josh and that would be that.

Wouldn't it?

So why didn't her plan seem to be quite so simple anymore?

Chapter Two

Her nephew, so far, hated her.

Okay, maybe that was an exaggeration. Maggie braced her arms on the kitchen counter and let her head fall forward with a sigh. Almost lunchtime on their very first day together and Cody hadn't spoken more than four words to her. And only *then* because she'd spoken to the little boy first. It would take time for him to adjust, this she knew. It didn't bother her. *Really.*

If only he wouldn't look at her like he might a particularly freaky bug. He edged around her like he expected her to squirt something vile at any moment.

She squared her shoulders and her resolve. She was not here in the capacity of auntie. To Cody, she was the nanny and a poor sub for Mrs. Herman at that.

The shrill of the phone snapped Maggie back to reality. She grabbed the handset off the counter. "Hello?"

"Maggie. It's Josh." Oh, Lord. Her insides did a totally unwelcome little flip. "How's everything going there so far?"

"Morning, Josh," she said, glad her voice remained steady. "We're doing just fine." True enough. Just not the kind of fine she'd hoped for.

"That's good." The relief in his voice rang in her ear. "Sorry I wasn't there this morning," he added. "I rotate on calls with two other docs. I usually get calls every night

I'm on. Not all of them involve me having to go in to the hospital, though."

"It's okay. I understand." She prowled around the kitchen. Talking to him on the phone wasn't much easier than doing it in person. Here he was right in her ear and she couldn't put distance between them.

"Is he right there?" Josh asked. "I'd like to talk to him for a minute."

Maggie headed for the stairs. "Of course. He's got his trains out in his room. Hold on."

She called for Cody, who came running when he heard it was his dad. After a brief chat, and numerous looks slid Maggie's way, from which she deduced the conversation was about her, Cody handed the phone to her and returned to his trains without a backward glance. She stared at his retreating form with a muffled sigh and lifted the handset to her ear.

"Josh? Still there?" The bright note in her voice sounded false, even to her.

"Yeah," he said, sounding distracted. "But I have to go. My next patient is here. Give Cody time, Maggie. He's a little shy. He'll come around."

"Of course he will. We really are doing fine here, Josh," she assured him. "I'm not worried." *Much.*

"Good. Listen, I'll give you a call later if it looks like I'll be late getting home." Maggie heard a female voice in the background and the rustle of paper.

"That's fine. See you then."

"Bye." *Click.*

The dial tone sounded in her ear. Maggie stood and stared at the phone for a second before replacing it in its cradle on the wall. She released a long breath. If she couldn't get a handle on this bizarre attraction to Josh, what would she do?

Maggie stalked over to the fridge and yanked open the door in search of lunch for Cody. "I know exactly what I'll do," she muttered as she pulled out sliced turkey. "I'll work harder to get over it."

She wasn't stupid enough to fall for her boss.

Again.

Josh tipped his chair back and stared at the ceiling of his office where he'd taken advantage of a few quiet moments to scarf lunch and call Maggie.

It's just because it's their first day alone. It didn't have anything to do with Maggie's long legs or that smooth, dark hair that fell in a thick mass past her shoulders. Nothing to do with those clear blue eyes, or the wariness with which she watched him. And, of course, he wasn't thinking about her because he was attracted to her.

Not at all.

She was the nanny for God's sake.

"Hey, Doc." Marta, his nurse, leaned in his office. "Julie Henney's ready in One."

Great. "Thanks. I'll be right there," he said, and let the chair legs thump forward onto the floor. He didn't think he'd ever seen Julie Henney for an actual illness, unless he considered her inability to take a hint a sickness.

"Everything all right?" Marta asked and Josh arched a brow.

"Of course. Why do you ask?" Marta possessed the finely tuned radar of a protective older sister, except she was younger and not related to him at all. Well, unless he counted the fact she'd married his best friend.

"You just seem a little distracted."

Josh shrugged. "No, everything's fine. Just Cody's first day with his new nanny, that's all." The truth as far as it went.

Marta nodded and seemed to accept it. Josh struck out for Exam One, where Julie Henney waited.

Before opening the door he grabbed her chart from the box and steeled himself. Ms. Henney had been after him for years. In fact, she'd offered him what she'd termed *comfort* not two months after Lucy's death. The memory still made his stomach turn.

The worst part? Lucy had considered Julie a good friend.

He pushed open the door and fixed what he hoped was a neutral expression on his face. He couldn't give an inch or she'd be all over him like he was a chocolate buffet. "Hi, Julie. What brings you here today?"

She perched on the end of the table, her skinny legs crossed at the ankle, her skirt stopping midthigh. She'd braced on her arms, leaning forward, no doubt to be sure he'd get an eyeful of what he knew to be artificially enhanced cleavage since he'd recommended the surgeon. Bottle blond hair loose and silky on her shoulders? Check. Pout firmly in place, predatory gleam in her pale blue eyes? Double check.

She must have broken up with her latest sugar daddy.

"Hey, Josh." Her voice was a throaty purr.

"Let's see." He made a show of examining Marta's few notes. "You're here for a sore throat?"

She shifted on the table. Probably to make sure he noticed her rack. "Yes."

Josh grabbed his laryngoscope and clicked it on. "Open up so I can see."

When he shone it down her throat—no redness, no drainage, no surprise—Julie grabbed his arm. She looped one foot around his leg and rubbed her hand on his chest. "I'm all fine now," she murmured. "Why don't you lock that door and ask me to open up again?"

Hell. Josh extricated himself from her grip and stepped back. Enough was enough. He'd been polite to Julie for years, out of respect for Lucy, and this woman never got the hint. He looked her straight in the eye.

"I've been nice about this for way too long," he said, keeping his voice cool. "I'm not interested in you, Julie. I'm not interested in anything you have to offer. I think it would be best if you found another doctor."

She turned purple and her jaw dropped then snapped shut. She sat up straight, tugged at the hem of her skirt. "Oh, come on, Josh. I didn't mean anything by it," she sputtered. "What's a little sex between friends? You're alone, I'm alone. Lonely. Why can't we enjoy each other?"

Josh inhaled a deep breath and hissed it out. Damn. "I'm not interested in a relationship," he said firmly. "Of any kind."

She shot up one manicured eyebrow. "I'm not looking for marriage, Josh. Are you still hung up on Lucy? She's been gone a long time. And you've been alone a long time—fine," she snapped and threw up her hands. "Fine. I get it. I'm outta here. If you change your mind—"

"I won't," Josh said. "It doesn't matter how long Lucy's been gone. She was my wife." *Not that I was much of a husband.* Josh shoved the thought and the accompanying pain away. "Do you want a recommendation for another physician?"

She slid off the table, her skirt slipping up so it barely covered her cheeks. She tugged it back down and grabbed her purse. "No. I do not. This is your loss, Doctor."

She sailed out, her chin up. Relief flooded him. He turned to gather up the paperwork. He'd been willing to keep her in his life out of respect for Lucy but clearly Julie's idea of respect and his were very different.

"Well, looks like that went well." Marta's dry voice came from behind him.

Josh turned and gave a half shrug. Actually, if it kept Julie from trying to jump him, he'd say it was a resounding success. "As well as it ever could, I guess."

She ripped off the paper cover on the table and began to unroll a new one. "That woman's had her eye on you for years."

Josh grunted. What could he say? "She was Lucy's friend. It just never seemed right."

She nodded. "You're a good guy, Doc. You'll find a good woman someday, too."

He gritted his teeth and turned on the water to wash up. "I'm not looking, Marta. You know that." Why couldn't people just leave him alone? Why was it so hard to believe he could be perfectly happy with just him and Cody? They were a team. They didn't need anyone else.

She studied him for a long moment and shrugged. "Maybe not. But sometimes, Fate does the looking for you."

Marta's words rang in his ears as he drove home that night, hard as he tried to ignore them. *Fate.* Was it Fate that had brought Maggie to them? He'd seen the glint in his mother's eye when he'd hired Maggie. Marta and half of Holden's Crossing—the half that wasn't trying to hook themselves or their single female relatives up with him—would undoubtedly have a similar look. A young, single, very attractive woman in his home. Conclusions would be drawn.

Too damn bad. Josh flexed his hands on the steering wheel. People could think whatever they wanted. He knew the truth, was fully aware every single moment of every single day of the promise he'd made to his dead wife. No one else knew, except his best friend. He'd made his bed, so to speak, after Lucy's death and stuck to his word for the past three years. He saw no reason to go back on it now.

Even if he was lonely.

Josh hissed and cranked the radio up as if the driving beat of Nickelback could squash that thought and all it implied. He'd never allowed himself to go there, to consider it. Cody was his first priority. Period.

The brightly lit house greeted him when he pulled in the driveway and he noticed smoke curled from the chimney. In the garage he caught a whiff of dinner from the kitchen. Did he smell a roast? He chuckled as he climbed out of his SUV. No doubt Cody would be relieved that a casserole wasn't on the menu tonight.

Maggie stood at the sink, her back to him as he came through the connecting door. Her long, dark ponytail fell down her back and the ties of her red apron draped over her shapely rear.

Not that it was the first place he looked or anything.

He turned to hang his keys on the rack and weather the tide of guilt that lapped at him. Had he ever walked in and simply appreciated Lucy's ass? No, he'd come in the house braced for a fight. Which she'd given him much more often than a smile.

Jeez, Luce, what a mess we were.

Maggie turned as he did. Her cheeks were flushed with the warmth of the kitchen and she offered him a quick smile.

"Dinner's almost ready. I just need to mash the potatoes. Cody's washing up." She lifted a steaming colander out of the sink and dumped it in a mixing bowl.

He walked up behind her, not too close, but enough to catch the scent of lavender off her hair. "Smells wonderful in here." God help him, he didn't mean just the food.

She tossed him a quick grin and scooted around him to the stand mixer. "Thanks. It's nothing fancy."

He headed to the powder room off the kitchen to wash up and get his unwelcome emotions back under control. Cram them back into the little box he imagined held all the things he didn't want to deal with.

Lately, the damned lid wouldn't stay closed.

When he reentered the kitchen, Cody was seated at the table. The little boy brightened and slid off his chair when he saw Josh. "Daddy!"

"Hey, big guy." Josh bent and pulled his son to him. The boy's skinny arms went around his neck and squeezed. Josh closed his eyes. He made the choices he did for Cody. It'd serve him well to remember that. "When we sit down, you can tell me all about your day, okay?"

Maggie set a plate at Cody's spot. "You're all set, Cody. I'll bring you some milk in a second. Josh, I'll get your plate now." She turned to go back into the kitchen.

He couldn't let her do that. He caught her wrist, felt the warmth of her skin through the fabric of her navy turtleneck. God, her bones were small. His fingers circled her wrist. She looked up at him, surprise on her face. "I'll get my own," he said, his voice a little rough in his throat.

"Um, well. Okay. I don't mind, though." She glanced down at her arm, still in his hand. He let go quickly, aware he'd held on to her a little too long.

Damn.

He filled a plate and sat down across from Cody, Maggie at his right. Not close enough to touch, but near enough that he was very aware of her presence. As he picked up his fork, one more thought in the guilt brigade hit him.

More often than not, he and Lucy hadn't eaten together. Other than holidays, he couldn't think of a single meal they'd shared with Cody that first year. He'd been too busy, or she'd been too angry. His appetite vanished.

"Josh? Is something wrong with the food?" Maggie's voice cut into his pity party. He looked up to see the concern on her face. He immediately felt bad. It wasn't fair to her for him to vanish down the mine-filled road of his past. He shook his head.

"No. Not at all. It smells amazing." He took a bite. Tasted that way, too. "So, Cody, what did you do today?"

Cody filled Josh in on his day. It seemed to him Maggie and his son had done all right. It took the little boy a while to warm up to people, but once he did he was a completely different child. Josh had a feeling Maggie would be seeing that kid soon.

"C'n I be 'scused?" Cody asked.

"Sure," Josh said. "Take your plate into the kitchen first. Be very careful."

"I will," Cody promised. Josh hid a grin as his son walked slowly around the table, his concentration on the plate and the utensils on it. A few seconds later he heard the clatter of the plate going in the sink. Maggie's eyes widened.

"I did it, Daddy!" Cody called. "C'n I go play now?"

Josh grinned at Maggie, who smiled back. "Yep."

"Yes!" And Cody was gone, all pumping legs and thumping stairs.

"We've got the clear-the-table part down pretty good," Josh said as he rose from his chair. "It's the delivery to the sink that we need to work on."

Maggie laughed. The clear, light sound floated over him, an unexpected balm to his frazzled emotions. "So I see." She pushed her chair back. "I'll take care of this."

He went to lay a hand on her arm, changed his mind. Better not to touch her. "I'll clean it up, Maggie," he said, but she shook her head. "Then let me help," he insisted as he gathered up dishes. "It's the least I can do. You rinse, I load."

She worried her lower lip for a second, then he saw her cave. "All right. Thank you. As long as you know it's not necessary."

"No thanks needed. It's the least I can do," he repeated.

In the kitchen, he rolled up his shirtsleeves and held out his hand for the first item. She handed him a plate.

"Cody seemed to have a good day," he said.

She nodded as she scraped the next dish. "Oh, he did. He's not too sure of me yet, but he's very sweet and wants to please. We'll get there. I'm not worried."

Josh slid a bowl into place. Something in her tone said she thought otherwise. "He can be shy. He'll come around."

"Of course he will. We didn't go out much today because I was trying to give him a little space. You know, to get used to me being in Mrs. Herman's place."

Worry zinged through him. "Was there something you needed that you couldn't get? You could have called me."

Her head came up, surprise in her blue eyes. Their color was nearly the same as Cody's. "Oh, no, Josh. We were fine. And your mom checked in on us, too, just in case. I won't bother you at work unless it's an emergency. I know how busy you are."

A bit of the scene with Julie flashed through his mind, only this time Maggie sat on the exam table in a short skirt and a come-hither look. His groin tightened at the possibilities.

For that, he'd have locked the door.

"Josh?" Amusement in her voice sliced across his fantasy, and he cleared his throat.

"I am busy. Most days are pretty crazy. But not so much so that if you guys are stuck somehow you can't call me."

Why was it so important that she know she could get him if she needed him? Because Lucy had complained so often that he was constantly unavailable when she needed something?

Because he wanted Maggie to think better of him than his wife ever had?

Maggie held out the last pan. "Don't worry, Josh. If I need you, I'll call." Her words and their double meaning hung in the air as her fingers touched his when he took the pan. Heat arced between them with the intensity of a live wire. His gaze caught hers for a heartbeat, before alarm sprang into her eyes. She quickly backed up, grabbed a washcloth and started swabbing the counter. He concentrated on fitting the last pan into place and closed the dishwasher, wondering how to break the suddenly awkward silence. What the hell was going on with him?

Maggie rinsed and folded the cloth, then draped it on the faucet. Not looking at him, she said, "If you don't need anything, I think I'll head upstairs. Do you need me to put Cody to bed?"

Josh shook his head. "As long as I don't get called, I'll do it."

She nodded. "Okay, then. Good night."

She turned and moved toward the stairs, her back perfectly straight. He doubted she'd take it too kindly if he swept her off her feet and carried her upstairs.

Tonight, anyway.

Shoving Josh and the kitchen weirdness out of her mind, Maggie paused in Cody's doorway. He didn't see her. With his back to her and his attention on his Matchbox cars, she figured she could drive a train through there and he wouldn't notice.

"Cody." He whipped his head around so hard his curls lifted and settled. "What are you playing?"

He poked at a fire truck. Paused for a moment. "Fireman."

"Ahhh." She leaned on the door frame. "Do you want to be a fireman someday?"

Cody shrugged, then nodded.

"That's good. Firemen help people."

"An' they drive big trucks," Cody observed, lifting one and studying it with one eye open.

Maggie hid a smile. Trust a kid to get to the heart of the matter. "That they do."

He returned to playing with his toys and she watched for a minute. The conversation was clearly over, but she loved the fact they'd actually had one. She slipped out of the room and into her own across the hall.

She closed the door and let her head fall against it with a soft thunk.

Holy cow. She'd had her first day as a nanny. As Cody's nanny.

While he wasn't too sure of her yet, she had to believe they'd get there. Josh seemed to think the little boy would come around soon enough.

Josh. A little shiver ran down up her spine. She needed to watch herself around him, make sure she hid the attraction she felt. Maybe it was just the fact he was a nice guy and loved his son—so different from her ex.

That was it. It had to be.

It couldn't be anything more.

Chapter Three

To distract herself, Maggie grabbed her cell off the night-stand, plopped in one of the chairs and dialed her best friend's number.

"Maggie!" Kerry didn't even bother with hello. "How did it go?"

Maggie filled her friend in on her day. "He needs to warm up to me still. He misses his old nanny a lot," she finished.

"Of course he does," Kerry agreed. "Poor little guy. He's been through so much."

"I know. It will take some time but he'll adjust," Maggie said, echoing what she'd told Josh earlier in the day. "Josh said he's a little shy."

Something in her tone gave her away. "Really," Kerry said, drawing out the word. "Josh, huh? Tell me about him."

Maggie mentally kicked herself for even getting into this. She stood up, walked to the sliding doors, her gaze on the pine trees in the backyard. The faint scent of burning leaves lingered on the breeze as she slid the door open. "There's not much to tell. As far as I can tell, he works hard and he adores his son."

"Sounds perfect," Kerry teased. "Is he hot?"

"Kerry! He's my boss." She kept her voice low, even though Josh wasn't likely to overhear.

Her friend sighed, all signs of teasing gone. "I know. I'm sorry. That didn't go so well for you last time."

"You could say that," she murmured, thinking of the baby that wasn't hers. "But I'd never get involved with him," she added. "It'd be way too weird and anyway, I'm here for Cody."

"So he is attractive," Kerry said.

An understatement, that. Maggie's fingers still tingled where they'd touched his. She curled her hand tighter around the phone. "Well, yeah. In a generic kind of way. You know. Not personally. To me." She rolled her eyes. She sounded a little too casual, even to her own ears.

Kerry paused and Maggie held her breath. "I see. Well, that's good. You don't want a repeat of Tony."

She exhaled. "God knows that's true. I'm here in a professional capacity, period. Cody is my focus."

No matter how unexpectedly attractive his father was.

"Of course he is," Kerry agreed. "Did you learn anything about Lucy?"

Kerry's question caused Maggie's conscience to give her jab. "No. Not yet. I don't feel comfortable bringing her up yet." It seemed like Josh should be the one to start that particular conversation. Maggie wasn't sure she could bring up Lucy and not blurt out the truth. Soon, but not yet. She wanted to let everything settle first and be sure it wouldn't be too hard on Josh and Cody to tell them who she was. It wasn't ideal, but she couldn't see another way to protect them.

"It's early," Kerry murmured. "I'm sure you'll get the chance. In the meantime, keep your eyes peeled for a good guy. Not all men are like Tony."

Maggie thought of Brian, her best friend's husband. "Of course they're not. You've got a good one."

Kerry laughed. "Oh, yes, I do. I really do. And we'll get you a good one, too. Trust me."

Maggie made a little humming noise. "We'll see. I'm sure not going to find him here. Holden's Crossing seems pretty small. I'm guessing the good ones are taken already. But I'm not in the market anyway." After her marriage, it seemed prudent to avoid all things commitment-related.

"Maybe, maybe not. Don't let Tony win," Kerry ordered. "Make sure it's because it's what *you* want. If you give up on all this, on ever being happy or a family of your own, you've let him win. He doesn't get to ruin your life."

Again. The unspoken word echoed in Maggie's head. She swiped at her now-moist eyes. "You're absolutely right. He doesn't. I'll keep my options open."

They chatted a few more minutes, then hung up. Maggie snapped her phone shut as Cody caught her attention, racing into the backyard with his dad behind him. Cody held a soccer ball, which he dropped on the ground and kicked toward his dad. His little-boy laugh floated in through the door. Josh kicked the ball back, then looked up. He waved. Caught, she couldn't exactly duck out of sight so she fluttered her fingers back.

"You play?" he called, and Maggie opened the door farther so she could step out on the balcony into the wood smoke–scented twilight. She crossed over to the railing and leaned on it, the wood cool through her sleeves.

"Not in years," she said as Cody gave the ball a solid kick. "Not since college."

"You can kick it around with us," he offered, and Maggie's chest squeezed at the invitation. "Right, Code?"

Cody darted a glance up at Maggie, then to his dad. He nodded and zeroed back in on the ball as it flew off Josh's foot. She was tempted, but she shook her head. "No thanks," she said to the top of Josh's head. No topside bald spot for him. "Maybe another time."

He executed some fancy footwork with the ball, indicating more than a passing relationship with the game of soccer. "Sounds good. We've got to go in soon, anyway. Almost bedtime for someone."

Cody's head came up. "It's not dark yet," he protested and Maggie smothered a laugh.

"Not yet," Josh agreed. "But it will be soon. Five more minutes, big guy, and it's time to hit the shower."

Maggie turned from the railing and walked back inside. While she could watch the two of them interact for hours, it probably wasn't a good idea. Keeping a distance was the best option.

Still, she left the door open to hear their voices and laughter, the thunk of the ball, as the sounds all drifted in on the chilly evening breeze.

Maggie spent the next two weeks doing an admirable job of ignoring the physical attraction she felt for Josh. Part of that had been keeping a bit of an emotional distance, developing a routine that worked for Cody but kept her out of incidental contact with Josh as much as possible. She kept her professionalism front and center.

Except for today.

Somehow she'd been roped into a family dinner.

Still not sure exactly how Ellen had gotten her to accept the invitation, Maggie stared out the window of Josh's SUV. The trees clipped by as she replayed the conversation in her head.

Dinner, Ellen had said. *Love to have you join us.*

When Maggie opened her mouth to decline she found herself accepting instead. An apparent disconnect of common sense and her tongue.

So here she sat with Josh and Cody on the way to El-len's. The whole thing blurred lines she'd been so careful to keep clear.

"Gramma has a dog," Cody announced into the silence. Josh had been very quiet. Thinking maybe of Lucy? She certainly was never far from Maggie's thoughts.

She half turned in her seat, grateful for the interruption. "She does? What kind?"

"A big one," Cody said, his gaze on the back of Josh's head. "Right, Daddy?"

"That's right," Josh agreed. He slid a glance her way. "Friendly, though. In case you were wondering."

"I like dogs," she said. "What's his name?"

"Riley," Cody said.

"That's a good name." She thought wistfully of Bear, the dog she'd shared with Tony. Bear had stayed with him. One more thing she'd surrendered to be free of the marriage.

"Are you okay over there?"

She blinked and looked over at Josh. "I'm fine. I used to have a dog," she blurted.

"Really?" Josh and Cody said in unison.

She was in it now. "Yes. His name is Bear."

"Where is he?" Cody asked.

"Well." *Here goes.* "He's with my, um, ex-husband."

Cody's eyes rounded and out of the corner of her eye Maggie saw Josh flex his hand on the steering wheel. A small ball of unease settled in her stomach. Had he known she was divorced? She'd told Ellen. She couldn't remember if it'd come up otherwise.

"Don't you miss him?"

She knew who Cody meant. "I miss Bear. I do." She'd never really missed Tony, only what they never really had. In retrospect, it said so much about her marriage. "He's a good dog, but an old one. We thought it was better for him to stay in his own familiar house."

"Gramma will share Riley. Right, Daddy?"

"Of course." Josh sent a quick smile her way.

Touched, Maggie smiled at each of them in turn. "Thank you. That's so sweet."

"You can meet him in a few." Josh turned onto a gravel drive. "We're here."

They wound through the trees for a short distance before opening up to a large lawn and a low ranch house. A big dog of any number of breeds loped across the grass, barking and wagging his entire rear end.

"That's Riley!" Cody cried as the SUV came to a stop. The little boy popped the seat belt on his car seat and jumped out the door to roll with the dog on the ground, the age-old greeting of little boys and big canines.

"Good thing it's not wet out," Josh commented as he and Maggie unbuckled.

"Would that stop him?" Maggie asked as she watched Riley lick Cody's face.

Josh paused, then grinned over at his son. "Not likely," he admitted. His keys slipped out of his hand and fell with a clank on the floor.

Since they landed on her side, Maggie leaned over and reached for them. Josh did the same and their heads bumped. She sat up. "Oh! Sorry."

"My fault." He leaned over and touched her forehead lightly. Her traitorous nerve endings gave a little zing. "You've got a bit of red mark here."

For a heartbeat, their gazes locked and her pulse skipped, then kicked up as the teasing in his eyes melted to heat. Awareness sparked between them, a quick flare. She could smell the spicy soap he'd used, the detergent on his clothes. She curled her hand around her purse strap, as if it could keep her from leaning over just a little farther to see what he tasted like.

A joyful bark broke the spell.

"Ah. Well, we'd better get inside," Josh said and nearly leaped out of the SUV.

She shut her eyes for a moment. The past two weeks had slipped by so smoothly. No awkward moments like this one, where the inappropriate attraction reared its ugly head. She'd managed to convince herself it had gone away.

So much for that.

Maggie inhaled deeply as she got out of the vehicle, as if the extra air would squish the butterflies that rioted in her belly. She needed to settle her pulse before she went in to face Josh's mother and the woman's very sharp eyes.

Before she could take two steps, Cody and Riley barreled around the front end of the SUV.

"This is Riley," Cody announced, his fingers trailing down the dog's spine. "Wanna pet him?"

Riley plunked his rear down in the gravel and wagged his tail. Maggie rubbed her hand between the dog's big ears. "He's a nice boy," she said. "Isn't he?"

"Yeah. He's my friend. C'mon, Riley, let's go play!" Boy and dog raced off.

She started toward the house and faltered. Josh stood between her and the door, hands in his pockets, his pensive gaze fixed where Cody and Riley had disappeared. For a wild second she wished she could go over and slip her arms around him, but that ended in a wave of guilt. She wanted to bang her head on the nearest hard surface. What was wrong with her? He couldn't be more off-limits, widowed or not. He'd been married to her half sister. The fact she'd never known Lucy didn't make it right.

* * *

Josh saw Maggie's indecision, appreciated it. Best if they forgot about the thing in the truck just now. If *he* forgot how badly he'd wanted to lean a little closer, capture her lips with his own. See if she tasted as sweet as she smelled.

Too bad it was impossible. Thinking how much Lucy would have loved to see Cody roughhousing with Riley put a quick damper on his inappropriate emotions.

He shook off the melancholy thoughts as Maggie closed the distance between them and tried to act normal.

"Like Riley?"

He sensed her relax a fraction. "I do. What is he, part shepherd?"

"And a lot of other things." They started walking again and Josh noted she kept a few extra inches between them. Just as well. "At the shelter, they weren't quite sure what all he had in him."

"A pedigree's not all it's cracked up to be." Her tone was light, but he caught an undertone of something darker in her words. Referring, maybe, to the ex-husband? That had been a bit of a shock. Not that she'd been married, but that some stupid guy had let her go.

Before he could formulate a reply, Ellen opened the front door and waved. "Hurry up, you two! Cody and Riley will eat all the cookies if you don't get in here."

"What, there's cookies? Before dinner? I'm there." Josh heard Maggie's soft giggle at his words and something that had been coiled tightly inside him loosened and warmed.

"Well, we've got company, and Halloween is two days away. Good excuse as any to bake." Ellen gave Maggie a quick hug before stepping aside. "Good to see you, honey. Come on in."

Josh followed the women inside, took Maggie's coat

and his own to the entry closet. He caught a whiff of her perfume, something light and fruity, from the shearling jacket she'd worn. He resisted the urge to bury his face in it and inhale.

So different from the heavy, provocative scents Lucy had favored.

He shoved the jackets in the closet and closed the door a little harder than necessary. Two things he knew. One, no more guilty comparisons allowed today. And two, leaving his matchmaking mother alone with Maggie for too long was not a good plan.

Later that evening, Maggie tied the laces of her running shoes, then leaned on the foyer wall to stretch her calves. She needed a good hard run to get the whole afternoon out of her system.

As enjoyable as it'd been, she couldn't shake the sense she'd been handpicked for Josh as much as Cody. Ellen, bless her, hadn't exactly been subtle with her comments and questions. The older woman clearly thought the time had come for her son to move on. Maggie knew she wasn't the right woman for Josh, even if she couldn't tell Ellen why.

He'd held her at arm's length all afternoon, clearly wanting to discourage his mother. It hadn't worked but it had helped Maggie feel better. Sort of. Considering they'd gone from that *moment* of…whatever it had been in the truck to being simply polite and civil. She felt a little whiplashed and it was her own fault.

So. She needed to clear her head.

She tugged down the hem of her bright pink hoodie and opened the front door. Josh and Cody had settled down in the family room to watch *Cars,* Cody's favorite movie. Their laughter and the buttery scent of fresh popcorn followed her outside even as she tried to quash the longing to join them.

She headed down the block, toward town, past houses all decked out for Halloween, with orange lights and scarily fun decorations. A few already sported carved pumpkins.

Josh's street ended three blocks down at the town square. Another block or so over and she'd be on the water. A trail did follow the lake, but since it was nearing dark she opted to stick to the sidewalks. She reveled in the heat of her muscles and the pound of her shoes as she fell into the familiar rhythm. She let her mind go blank and just enjoyed the moment, the bite of the evening air, the breeze on her face, the bounce of her ponytail on her back.

Four miles later, she spotted another jogger on the same course, coming at her. She dropped to a cool-down walk as the other person approached. Maggie recognized her as the woman who lived down the block from Josh in the house that was undergoing a renovation.

"Hi," she said, and the other woman smiled and swung around to walk with her.

"Hi. We finally meet, I see." She held out one paint-splattered hand. "It's dry, I promise," she added with a laugh. "I'm Hannah McKay. I meant to get down and introduce myself earlier but I've been swamped."

"Maggie Thelan." She released Hannah's hand and shoved a damp tendril of hair off her forehead. "Cody Tanner's nanny. Do you know the Tanners?"

Hannah nodded. "I do. Mrs. Herman used to bring Cody down to the park on the corner almost every day."

"We haven't made it there yet, but I plan to. You're remodeling?"

Hannah blew out a breath. "I am. I'm hoping to turn it

into a bed-and-breakfast by next summer. It needs...well, it needs some love. No other way to put it."

Maggie pictured the imposing structure with its peeling paint and sagging porch. "I guess it does."

Hannah followed her train of thought. "The outside looks scary, but it's in better condition than you think. Anytime you have a few extra moments you should stop over and I'll show you. I can always use another perspective. Not to mention the help."

"I'd like that," Maggie said, delighted. "Are you doing this all by yourself?"

Hannah closed her eyes for an instant. "Yes. Yes, I am," she said. "Anyway, just knock. I'm always there. Except for when I'm at the home center," she added thoughtfully. "Which seems to take a good amount of my time. And money."

Maggie laughed. "Yeah, I bet."

"All right then. I'm serious. Come down anytime."

The prospect of a friend was heartening. "You know, I just might take you up on that."

"Please do. It was really nice to finally meet you." Hannah gave a little wave and turned around to continue on her run, her short blond ponytail bouncing. Maggie continued to head for home, her heart a little lighter.

In the driveway, she stretched out before entering the house. The noise of the movie carried clearly from the family room. She toed off her shoes and put them in the closet. With any luck, she could just sneak up the stairs and escape into her room without having to face Josh or the disturbing fact she'd nearly kissed him this afternoon.

"How was your run?"

Maggie jumped at Josh's quiet voice. He stood in the shadow of the hallway, outside the kitchen. Great. Here she stood, sweaty and gross—she stopped the thought. It didn't matter. He was off-limits, no matter what his mother's intentions were, or how much she wished circumstances could be different. "Oh, fine. It's a lovely night. I met Hannah down the street."

"That's good. Mrs. Herman liked her a lot." He hesitated. "Do you want to join Cody and me? We've got way more popcorn then we'll ever eat." He tipped the full popcorn bowl slightly in her direction.

Yes. The single word danced on the end of her tongue, but she bit it back. "Thanks, but not tonight." But oh, she wished she could.

Even in the dim light of the foyer, she saw both relief and disappointment flash across his face, echoing what was warring inside her. She wasn't sure if it made her feel better or worse to know he might be struggling with the same thing she was.

"Another time maybe." He gave her a nod and turned to go in the living room.

"Maybe," she echoed but knew she'd avoid it if she'd learned anything from their near-miss kiss that afternoon. Still, as she ran up the stairs, she couldn't suppress a little shiver at how close they'd come, or the disappointment they'd been interrupted.

She wasn't sure which one was more dangerous.

Chapter Four

"I'm sorry, Maggie, I'm running a little behind." Josh's harried voice carried clearly over the phone the next evening. "I know it's pumpkin-carving night. I'll be there as soon as I can."

Maggie pulled two plates out of the cupboard. "It's okay. It happens. We'll wait for you."

"If I'm going to be more than an hour I'll call again. Then you can start without me." Voices in the background, then Josh spoke again. "Gotta run. See you later."

"Okay. Bye." She hung up, turned to find Cody standing behind her.

"Was that my daddy?" he asked.

She reached out and touched his soft curls. He didn't step away the way he would have a week ago. Her heart warmed. "Yep. He's going to be a little late. We'll go ahead and eat, okay? Then maybe we can get stuff set up so you and your dad can carve the pumpkins."

After dinner and kitchen cleanup, Cody divided his time between the front window and the pumpkins lined up on the kitchen floor. So Maggie took matters into her own hands.

"Let's get ready to carve. We can get the newspaper spread out to keep the floor clean," she told Cody as she pulled a bunch of papers out of the recycle pile. "And we can start cleaning the pumpkins out. That way, when your dad gets here, you guys can start carving right away. Okay?"

Cody sent a lingering look at the door. "Okay," he said with a dramatic sigh. She suppressed a smile.

"He'll be here soon," she assured the little boy and handed him a folded section of newspaper. "Open it like this, and lay it down. We'll need a couple of layers."

Josh walked in as they finished spreading the newspapers on part of the tile floor. Cody hurried over to greet him.

"Hi, Daddy! Look! We put papers down to keep the punkin stuff off the floor. And Maggie brought the punkins in so they wouldn't get cold," he added.

Josh tugged at his tie and arched his brow at Maggie. "Really? I didn't know pumpkins got cold." Despite his teasing tone, he looked tired. His hair was slightly mussed as if he'd thrust his fingers through it more than once. Her fingers itched to smooth it back down.

She gave him a little smile instead and kept her voice steady. "Well, they do inside. No way am I sticking my hand in a freezing cold pumpkin."

Josh chuckled. "Good point."

"Maggie said she'd make the seeds so we could eat 'em when we're done," Cody said.

"We'll roast them. They make a yummy snack," she explained.

"Sounds good. I'm going to go change. Be right back," Josh said as he tugged the tails of his shirt out of the waist of his chinos. Maggie caught a glimpse of smooth skin and taut abs and her mouth went dry.

Then she gave herself a mental slap. Really? A teeny glimpse of skin was all it took to get her hormones fired up? Sheesh. She squeezed her eyes shut for a second, then shifted her attention to the little boy sitting by the pumpkins. He was her focus. Definitely not his father.

"Okay, Cody," she said brightly. "Which one is yours again?"

She knew, of course, because he'd told her several times the biggest pumpkin was his. But she asked the question anyway since it guaranteed an excited response.

Cody patted the huge pumpkin. It hit him midthigh. "This one!" he said with glee.

Maggie smiled and pretended to slap her forehead. "Of course that's yours. What was I thinking? Are you ready to help me clean it out?" She wrangled it onto the newspaper. Despite sitting in the house for the better part of the day, its smooth skin was cold under her hands. "Whew! This is awfully heavy, Cody. I bet it has a lot of seeds. Let's see, okay?"

Cody did a little dance. "Yeah! I want to see."

Josh reentered the kitchen. She looked up and managed to hold on to her smile when she took stock of him. Faded jeans, worn T-shirt, bare feet. She managed not to lick her lips and forced her attention back to the task at hand. "You're just in time."

He held her gaze just a fraction too long, then dropped away. She was afraid she'd glimpsed regret in his gaze. For what? He cleared his throat. "That's good. I'm glad I made it. I wouldn't want to miss this. Can I help?"

"Yes." She held out her hand, pleased it stayed steady, in mock imitation of a surgeon. "Scalpel, please."

His mouth twitched as he grabbed the pumpkin-carving tool off the counter and slapped it in her palm. "Check."

She plunged the tool into the top of the pumpkin and sawed it around the crown. The rich, fresh scent of the fruit rose up and little bits of the shell went flying. Cody watched, leaning on his father, eyes huge. When she whipped the top off with a triumphant flourish, Josh grinned and nudged Cody.

"She doesn't mess around, does she?"

Cody grinned back. "Can we carve it now?"

Maggie shook her head. "We have to clean it out, remember?" She tipped the pumpkin toward him. "Look at all the seeds. Let's get them out of here. You want to help? Then you and your dad can start carving."

Cody kneeled beside her and she handed him a pasta spoon with a smile. He returned her smile, then said softly, "I want to carve it with you."

Maggie couldn't breathe, caught in the little boy's earnest bright blue eyes. Tears burned in her throat as her gaze flew to Josh, who wore a small smile, then back to his son. She swallowed the lump in her throat and smiled at her nephew. "Then we'd better get cracking, don't you think?"

Later that night Maggie sat on the front porch step, bathed in the glow of the orange twinkle lights strung on the porch railing. The full moon's silvery cast provided additional light. She pulled a soft fleece throw tighter around her shoulders to ward off the evening chill. The carved pumpkins, all three of them, flickered at her feet.

Progress. She'd made it tonight with Cody. He'd wanted to give her a hug—finally—before he went to bed. A little shiver of joy slipped through her. She could still feel those strong little-boy arms around her neck.

From a nanny point of view, she figured he finally felt comfortable with her. That was a huge step, one she'd been waiting anxiously for. From the auntie point of view—well, he'd hugged her. A small smile tugged at her lips and she tipped her head up to look at the stars. What could be better?

Behind her the door opened and closed with a soft snick.

She tensed as Josh eased himself down beside her, and willed the totally inappropriate warmth away. Being his employee was enough to make him off-limits. She couldn't afford to make that mistake again.

Being her former brother-in-law sent it out of the park.

"I think you won Cody over tonight," he said, his words accompanied with a puff of breath on the chilly air.

Pleasure slid through her and she smiled. "Not many kids, especially little boys, can resist the opportunity to get slimy."

"True." He draped his forearms on his knees with a low chuckle that heated Maggie in places she didn't want to name. "For some of us, it never goes away."

She laughed, started to rise. Best not to be out here with him too long. "Boys will be boys, I guess. Well, it's late. I'm going to head in."

He reached out and snagged her wrist. Her nerve endings briefly sizzled and she resisted the urge to yank her arm away. Her gaze locked on his. Even in the dim light she saw pain and pleading there. Her breath caught.

"Stay. Please. For a minute. If you're cold we can go in. I just— I want to tell you a little bit about Cody's mom. About what happened."

Maggie stopped breathing. She sank back down carefully, as if moving too fast would shatter the moment and send it skittering out of her reach, like marbles on a hard floor.

"Okay," she said, relieved her voice sounded normal. She chanced a peek at him, saw in the soft light the hard set of his jaw. She could almost feel the waves of tension rolling off him. Her belly clenched in response and she linked her fingers together tightly to keep them from shaking.

He scrubbed a hand over his face and Maggie held her

breath, afraid to give away how badly she wanted to know. Why she wanted to know.

"This is hard," he admitted, his voice rough. "I don't talk about Lucy much. A lot happened after her death." He stared down at the step, seeming to wrestle with something internally, and Maggie's heart cracked. "I won't burden you with the details. Suffice it to say her parents blamed me. But whatever our issues were, Lucy loved Cody. More than anything. She was a good mom. When I realized she wasn't going to make it after the—the accident, I promised her I'd put Cody first, before *anything* and everything else. I don't know if she heard me, but it's a promise I've honored for almost four years. It's the least I can do for her. And for Cody."

Maggie swallowed. She heard both the warning and the regret in his voice. He'd made a vow and intended to keep it. She could understand and respect that, and she would. But still, there was no blame here.

She laid her hand on his arm and tried for diplomacy. "Josh, it's not your fault she died. How could they think that?" A snowy night, the newspaper article had said, and the car hit a tree. Lucy had been the only occupant in the vehicle.

In the cold wash of the silver moon, she saw his features go even harder. The rough wool of his jacket scraped her hand when he pulled his arm away and stood up. "Because it's the truth." The rawness in his voice sliced across her soul. "Her family wants nothing to do with me. Sad to say, it's mutual. I'm sorry I brought it up, Maggie. Not sure what I was thinking. Forget I said anything."

Maggie squeezed her eyes shut against the burn of tears as he crossed the porch and closed the door behind him with a slight bang. She dropped her head to her knees as the tears made hot tracks down her cold cheeks.

Her family wants nothing to do with me.

Her stomach rolled, both at the words and the pain behind them. What a horrible situation for all of them. Her heart ached.

A terrible thought hit her. He wanted nothing to do with Lucy's family. If he found out she was technically family...

He'd fire her and she'd lose her only connection to Cody and Lucy.

She sucked in a breath, the chilly air burning her lungs, and swiped at her wet cheeks. Her secret, and the choice she'd made to keep it, weighed on her more than ever. She'd made a hell of a mess of her good intentions.

Where did she go from here?

Josh avoided Maggie as much as possible over the next few days, given they lived in the same house. That she cared for his son. That they ate meals together. It made things a little tricky but it was better than examining why he'd felt compelled to try and explain the whole Lucy thing.

How I failed her. Though he figured he'd made that pretty clear.

On the other hand, hadn't he intended to make clear why he was off-limits? Not that she'd pushed anything. He seemed to be the one struggling with this attraction thing. It had been a stupid lapse on his part.

"You and Cody still on for tonight?" Marta's voice shattered his thoughts.

"Yeah. Cody can't wait to spend the night. He's talked about it all week." Normally, Josh looked forward to the poker game he played with Travis and a couple of their buddies once a month. Cody stayed at Trav's house with Marta and their son JT. Tonight he anticipated it for a completely different reason—it'd be legitimate time away from Maggie and her big blue eyes and all the temptations he'd shut himself off from. Things he hadn't even known he'd missed, that really he'd never had with Lucy. He didn't want to look at Maggie and see possibilities. It was too hard.

"So has JT." Marta studied him, then seemed to rethink whatever she'd been about to say. Instead, she swung her bag on her shoulder. "We'll see you in an hour or so."

"Yep. See you then."

Marta left and Josh pulled his stethoscope from around his neck and tossed it on his desk. He'd lock up, then stop on the way home for a six-pack. Maggie would have dinner ready and then he'd take his son and escape his own house.

Cody chattered nonstop the whole way to Marta and Travis's house. Nothing out of the ordinary there. He enjoyed listening to the little guy talk. Josh turned into the driveway and Cody leaned over to peer out his window.

"I see him! I see JT!" he cried, and Josh laughed.

"I see him, too," he said, waving at the little boy in the picture window. "Let's get you inside."

November had ushered in much colder, rainier weather and tonight was no exception. A few hard pellets of snow fell with the rain, tossed around by the brisk breeze. Josh opened Cody's door, grabbed his son's backpack and hurried behind him to the house. Marta had the door open before they even got on the porch. She closed it behind them as Cody and JT greeted each other with much excitement, then Cody shouldered his backpack and started to follow his friend.

"Hang on, Code." Josh caught his son by the pack's strap. "Give me a hug. I'll see you tomorrow morning."

Cody hugged him hard and Josh inhaled the sweet scent of his son. "Okay, Daddy. Love you."

"Love you, too." Josh ruffled Cody's curls affectionately and watched as his boy hurried after JT. Josh turned to Marta, who looked at him with amusement. "What?"

"You're such a good dad," she said.

He arched his brow, feigning hurt. "What? That's a surprise?"

She laughed. "Of course not. Not to me, anyway."

Josh frowned, serious now. "What do you mean?"

"I mean you seem to think sometimes you aren't. You're too busy, he has a nanny, whatever. But the time you do spend with him, you make really count." She punched him lightly on the arm. "Just an observation. Trav is in the garage. Don't worry about Cody. He'll be fine."

"I know he will. Thanks, Marta." Josh walked through the house to the back door. He could hear JT and Cody laughing and the sound made him smile as he left the house and jogged around to the garage. He wasn't completely sure he believed Marta as far as being a good dad went. After all, Cody didn't have a mom anymore—but he did try to be as present as possible for his son. When he wasn't half-tangled in knots over the nanny, of course.

He wasn't going any further down that road.

Travis glanced up as Josh entered the garage. "Give me a sec, then we'll go."

"No problem. We've got time."

He waited while Trav finished up. Always, his friend tinkered with engines. This time, he had the hood up on his wife's car. That same dedication made him an excellent mechanic and his garage so successful.

Trav dropped the hood with a thunk and washed up at the sink in the corner of the heated garage, then grabbed his jacket off the hood of his truck. "Ready to play?"

"I am," Josh agreed.

"Where's the nanny?"

"She has the night off." Josh hoped Trav would leave

it at that. Both men got in the SUV and Josh turned the engine over.

A pause. "So if she's got the night off, why are you hanging with us?"

"It's game night," Josh said. He tried not to think of the awkward dinner they'd endured. While polite, she'd said as little as possible to him. Both of them had focused on Cody. When he'd left the house, she'd given Cody a hug.

He got a polite nod and she wished him luck.

"Let me get this straight," Travis said as if Josh was somehow incapable of grasping the obvious. "You've got a gorgeous single woman under your roof and a place for Cody to go for the night. And you are going to hang out with the guys." He shook his head.

Without thinking, Josh said, "How do you know she's single and gorgeous? Where did you see her?"

Trav sent him a "gotcha" grin. "I didn't know. Until now."

Caught, Josh bristled. "It's not like that. You of all people know why I'm not going there. On top of that, Maggie works for me. She's great with Cody. I'm not going to screw that up." Any more than he already had.

Trav sighed. "I know, man. I know. I just wish…" He trailed off.

"What?"

His friend took a minute before answering. "That you'd give yourself a chance. Or, I guess, let yourself have a chance. If it's not Maggie, fine. But what happens when you meet someone and you want to pursue it?"

Josh's insides twisted. "I won't." He sounded more resolute than he felt.

Travis was silent for a long moment, then said, "Have it your way."

Josh didn't answer. A hollow feeling filled his chest. For

the first time he wondered if keeping his promise to Lucy was possible. Could he continue to put aside his needs, his life, as penance for the loss of hers? He'd been so careful for the past three years to avoid any kind of possible romantic entanglement. It hadn't been difficult. Now he had a potential one living under his roof.

He tried to call up Lucy's face, but her dark hair and blue eyes morphed into Maggie's. He stifled a groan as he turned into the driveway of their buddy's house. He needed to focus on what was really important here, which was Cody and his well-being. Trav was wrong. He wouldn't be pursuing anyone. Cody needed him. All of him.

He'd do well to remember that.

Maggie clicked the dishwasher on and leaned back on the counter. Normally, she'd enjoy an evening to herself, take the opportunity to have a hot bath and read a good book. But tonight, she was restless. Her mind kept cycling back to Josh and what he'd told her about Lucy and her family.

And she still didn't know what to do about it.

Her heart ached for both Lucy and Josh. For his pain and loss and guilt. With her own.

Unable to stay in the house, she grabbed her coat. From the front window, she could see lights were on in Hannah's house. Decision made, she headed out the door, into the cold.

Hannah answered on the third knock. Her eyes widened when she saw Maggie standing there, and a big smile lit her gorgeous face. "Yay! You came! Come on in," she invited and stepped back out of the doorway. "It's nasty out there."

"It is," Maggie agreed. "Do you need help with anything tonight? I would have called but I didn't have your number."

"Oh, trust me, you're fine," Hannah assured her. "I can always use the help. I've got a lot of rooms to scrape and paint. Most of them have some kind of weird peeling wallpaper. So there's always something."

Maggie stepped inside the foyer and peered with interest into the cozy room just off it. Two couches in what looked like dark green velvet, deep leather club chairs and a dancing fire made it inviting. "This room is lovely. It feels so warm."

Hannah beamed. "Thanks. I did it first—it didn't need much—but I needed something to show myself what it *could* look like. One room that wasn't chaotic or torn up or unfinished or ugly. So it's my inspiration room. It helps me keep plugging away." She pointed at a coat tree by the door. "You can hang your jacket there. I'll show you where I'm working."

Maggie hung her coat and followed Hannah up the stairs, which featured a carved handrail and a dark stain. Nearly every tread creaked under her feet. At the top of the stairs, Hannah walked a little way down the hall and stopped at a doorway with light spilling out of it. "I gotta warn you," she said with a grin, "this is a particularly bad example of nineteen-seventies wallpaper."

Maggie followed her into the room and laughed at the garish gold, brown and green print of people standing by a pond. "Oh, who thought these things up? And why would anyone ever think this would be a tasteful print to relax by?"

Hannah shook her head and shrugged. "I've been wondering that myself. There have been some doozies of weird wallpapers in this house. But this will make for a good 'before' print in my scrapbook. I mean, anything I do from here is an improvement."

Hannah showed Maggie how to apply the homemade

wallpaper solvent, peel the paper and scrape any stubborn residue. With the radio on low, tuned to a local soft rock station, they worked without speaking for a few minutes.

"So," Hannah said, "what brought you to Holden's Crossing?"

Maggie tensed. She didn't want to lie to Hannah. But could she trust the other woman?

Chapter Five

"A very messy divorce," Maggie said after a small pause. It certainly was true. The divorce had been rough. Being cast aside for another woman was never easy. But without the divorce, she wouldn't have come here.

Hannah sat back on her heels and regarded Maggie with sympathy. "Oh, I'm sorry to hear that. What happened? You don't have to talk about it, of course," she added quickly.

"It's okay. I don't mind. He cheated. And started a family with someone else." How odd those few words could encapsulate the deed that tore apart her life. And yet she could say them so calmly. "I lost my job when we divorced, since he had pull with my boss. I was a fourth-grade teacher. It was just easier to move." To get away from the whispers and the pitying looks. To get away from *him*.

Hannah covered her mouth with her hand. "I'm so sorry. That's awful."

Maggie nodded. "Yeah, it was. But it's working out okay. I just needed a new start, I guess." For lots of reasons.

"I hear you. This is a new start for me, too."

"A pretty ambitious one," Maggie commented, glad to switch the focus from herself. She pulled on the dampened paper and it peeled off in a small section.

Hannah tapped her scraper on the wall. "It is. But it's exactly what I needed to start over." She shrugged. "I'm divorced, too. Like you, it wasn't a nice one. I bought this house right afterward with my settlement. Anyway. How's it going with Josh?"

Maggie bit back a sigh. "Fine. He's nice enough, good to work for, and he's a fantastic dad to Cody." All nice, neutral facts. She doubted she could get anything so bland past Hannah much longer.

"Uh-huh. And one of Holden's Crossing's most eligible bachelors." A teasing note entered Hannah's voice. "I think nearly every woman in town has either thrown herself or a single female relative at his feet."

Maggie's grip on the scraper slipped as her stomach plummeted. This was news. "Seriously? I didn't get the impression he's a player." She knew for a fact he wasn't.

"Oh, no." Hannah shook her head and laughed. "He's not. He just steps over their bodies and keeps on going. There are a few, though, who have decided if he wants to date again it's going to be them. So you might want to watch out."

Startled, Maggie turned to look at her friend. "Me? Why?"

Hannah shrugged and slapped more solvent on the wall. "Because you live with him. Because you are young and gorgeous and because, as far as they can see, you're single. That makes you a target and an enemy. And, trust me, there are a couple of women here who will look at you exactly that way."

Maggie bit back a sigh. "Great. I'm just Cody's nanny. God knows I'm not looking for anything more. My last relationship was bad enough. Why would I ever want to go through that again?"

Hannah slanted her a look. "Because you found the right man this time. It happens. And I'm just giving you a heads-up on this."

"Lovely," Maggie said grimly. A cold thought gripped her. What if someone were to explore her background? Could her relationship to Lucy come up? Then she realized Hannah was speaking. "I'm sorry. What was that?"

"I just said not to worry about it too much. Josh can take care of himself, and you can, too. I just didn't want you to be surprised if some kitty-cat claws come your way when you didn't expect it."

"Thanks for the warning," Maggie said drily.

Hannah grinned. "No problem. What are friends for?"

Maggie left Hannah's at ten. Later than she'd planned, but hopefully still early enough to avoid Josh.

No more awkward run-ins, thank you very much. The past few days had been bad enough, what with his clear worry over what he'd told her and her own fear and guilt. This definitely hadn't turned out the way she'd planned when she'd come here.

Leaves crunched under her feet as she walked. She shoved her hands in her coat pockets and tilted her head back to look at the stars. Even with the streetlights, they were a bright sparkle on the night sky.

A swoop of lights and an engine caught her attention. Her heartbeat picked up. It couldn't be Josh. He was playing poker with his buddies. Would they really end this early?

Yes, they would. Maggie slowed her pace when the SUV pulled into Josh's driveway. Too late—he had to have seen her, since she was only two houses away. As tempting as it was, she couldn't exactly dive into the neighbor's shrubbery.

He parked in the driveway, got out and leaned on the truck, watching her approach. Maggie's pulse kicked up even higher and she kept her hands balled into fists in her pockets. They'd barely spoken all week, which was fine with her. Now, when Cody was no longer there to buffer them, he wanted to talk?

How cruel was that?

Josh pushed off the truck as she stepped into the driveway. His features were thrown into shadow by the nearby streetlight that leaked through the pine trees. She could feel the intensity of his gaze on her. She didn't speak, couldn't seem to get anything out of her throat.

"Hi," he said. His voice was low, but in the silence of the night it might as well have been a roar.

"Hi," she managed to respond. She stopped in front of him, unable to simply go on by. Awkwardness or not, he was her employer. And she didn't want him to know how he affected her.

"Out for a walk?"

"Not really. I just came from Hannah's. Spent some time removing ugly wallpaper." Her heart beat fast, but her voice was calm. That was good.

He nodded. "She's got quite a project down there." He stepped closer and she inhaled sharply. "I owe you an apology," he murmured. Her traitorous feet wouldn't move, wouldn't take the backward step her brain screamed she should take.

"Really? For what?" He was close enough now she could smell his leather jacket, his scent. The little shiver that ran up her spine had nothing to do with the chill of the night.

He scooped a lock of her hair back over her shoulder, his fingers brushing her cheek. The heat from the caress shot straight down. If she leaned forward just a little bit, she could touch him. This time she did step back and willed her knees to hold her. He cleared his throat and jingled his keys.

"For acting the way I have this week. My marriage to Lucy and the problems with her family have nothing to do with you. I'm sorry for getting personal. I crossed the line."

All the sparkly hormones ignited by his nearness curled up and died in the aftermath of his words. Now she felt the evening's cold, and a darker chill deep inside. She forced the words out through wooden lips. "It's okay, Josh. There's no apology needed." On the contrary, she should thank him. He'd given her the dose of reality she needed. How quickly she forgot who she was. She stepped around him and headed for the house.

He followed silently. Casting around for something to say, she asked, "How did the game go?"

He slid the key into the lock and opened the door. "Not my best night."

When he didn't say more, Maggie slid off her boots and coat. "Sorry to hear that. Well, I'm going to take a shower and see if I can get this wallpaper paste off me and out of my hair." She turned, intending a bright smile, but unable to summon it. "See you in the morning."

Josh's gaze darkened for a moment. "Have a nice shower."

His voice was low, a little rough. And his eyes were hot, hot enough to make Maggie nearly choke. "I will, thanks." She turned and sped up the stairs before she did something truly stupid.

Like invite him to wash her hair.

The next morning, Maggie stared in the fridge and her heart sank.

Right there, front and center next to the milk, sat the small cooler Josh used for his lunch.

Somehow, he'd left without it. That meant a trip to the office to drop it off. *He could just fend for himself.* Maggie sighed, pulled the cooler out and closed the fridge. Of course he could. But that wasn't fair, just because things were weird between them, to not help him out. She was a big girl. She and Cody could just drop it off. In, out and back home. Easy.

She walked to the bottom of the stairs. "Cody! Come get your shoes on," she called. Josh's nurse had dropped him off on her way to work a little while ago.

"Okay!" he yelled back, thumping out of his room and hitting the stairs in the full slide that made her heart stop. "Where we goin'?"

Maggie pointed to the cooler on the counter. "We're going to your dad's office. He forgot his lunch."

"Cool." Cody ground his feet into his light-up Thomas the Tank Engine sneakers and shrugged into his jacket. She opened the door to the garage and they trooped out to her car.

Maggie handed the cooler to Cody after she buckled him in. "Can you hang on to this while I drive?"

Cody nodded solemnly. "I won't let it fall," he said.

Maggie smiled. "I know you won't. Okay, let's hit the road."

Cody held the cooler on his lap while Maggie drove the short distance to the outskirts of town, where Josh's practice was located. The parking lot held several cars, and Maggie realized she didn't actually know how many people worked at the clinic. In the time she'd worked for Josh, she'd never been here.

Pushing through the doors, they entered a bright reception area, currently decorated in a fall theme with mums and pumpkins. An older woman in bright pink scrubs sitting behind a high counter looked up as they approached. "Can I help you?" she asked, her tone friendly.

Maggie rested her hand on Cody's back. "We're here to see Dr. Tanner."

"Okay. When is your appointment?" the woman asked, already reaching for the pile of files nearby.

"I'm sorry, I should have been more clear. I've got Cody Tanner here. I'm his nanny."

The woman stood up and peered over the counter. "Why, Mr. Cody Tanner! How nice to see you, young man. And you must be Maggie," she added, extending her hand over the counter. "I'm Teresa. You two can come on back and wait in his office."

Maggie opened her mouth to refuse but Cody was already walking toward the door, cooler banging on his leg. "Okay. As long as it's no trouble."

Teresa gave Maggie a quick, assessing glance. "Oh, it's no trouble, young lady. None at all. He'll be happy to see you." The last was directed at Cody, who launched into a description of a video game he'd played at JT's last night.

Maggie tamped down her nerves as they followed Teresa though the bustle and maze of short hallways, past several doors.

"His is the third door on the right," Teresa said. "Cody, stop by on the way out. I might have a treat for you."

"All right!" Cody boomed and Maggie had to smile.

"Cody!" A young woman with dark hair and a dazzling smile turned from the nurses' station before they could pass and bent to give him a quick hug. Maggie recognized her as the woman who'd dropped Cody off that morning. They'd exchanged waves but no actual words. "Good morning again. Here to see your daddy?"

"Daddy forgotted his lunch." Cody held up the cooler. "So me an' Maggie brought it to him."

"Oh." The speculation in the drawn-out word was nearly enough to send Maggie back to the car. She met the other woman's gaze squarely and the smile got even wider. "It's about time I got to officially meet you. I'm Marta. Josh is my husband's best friend."

Maggie returned the smile. "Nice to meet you. Josh has mentioned you and your family several times." Then she nearly winced. Her words implied a familiar relationship, not a professional one.

The curiosity in Marta's dark eyes was rampant, but she said nothing as she took a few more steps and opened a door. "Josh's office. I'm sure Teresa told him you're here. Code, I've got to run, but I'll see you later, 'kay?" To Maggie she offered a quick smile. "Nice to meet you." Then she hurried off, paperwork in hand.

Cody ran across the room and sat in his dad's swivel chair, swinging his legs, the cooler on the floor next to him. Maggie moved over to stand behind him and studied the pictures on the desk.

Cody, Ellen with Cody, Josh with Cody. No hint, of course, of Lucy. Frustration welled inside her. Why were there no pictures of Cody's mother? Had things been so bad Josh felt he had to wipe her out of his life? Or were the memories too painful to bear? After their conversation the other day, she leaned toward the latter.

The door opened and Josh stood framed in the doorway, his tie slightly askew, like he'd been tugging on the knot. Come to think of it, had she ever seen him with a perfectly straight tie?

"Hey, guys," he said, the warmth of his smile fading slightly he included her. It stung, even though she knew it was for the best. "What brings you here?"

Cody slid off the chair and skipped to his father. He wrapped his arms around Josh's legs. "We brought you lunch, Daddy! You forgotted it."

Josh shook his head. "I did, didn't I?"

Cody nodded. "Good thing Maggie looked in the 'frig-erator. She saw it and now we're here!"

Josh rubbed his hand across Cody's curls. His gaze caught Maggie's for a second and she held her breath. "Yes, you are. Thank you."

Maggie looked away, focused on the diplomas on the wall. He'd graduated from Michigan State University, same as she had. "It was nothing." The office was small and he seemed to take up all the oxygen, making it hard for her to breathe.

Had he spent a sleepless, restless night the way she had? Had he been hyperaware of her, just a few feet away, walls and door notwithstanding, the way she'd been of him? She didn't think she could handle the answer.

"Well, we'll get out of your hair," Maggie said too brightly. "Glad we got here in time. Ready, Cody?"

"Yeah, I've got patients. Trying to stay on schedule." He bent and pulled his son into a hug, and when her heart squeezed, Maggie wondered if she'd ever be unaffected by the sight. "Code, why don't you go back up to Teresa, and ask her for a sucker? If Maggie says it's okay, you can even have it before lunch." He looked up at Maggie and she nodded, startled he'd included her.

Cody swung his gaze to Maggie and she smiled. "Of course."

"Yes!" Cody pumped his fist as he hurried out the door.

"I'd better go with him." She started to follow but he caught her hand. She jumped and tried to ignore the licks of heat his touch sent through her.

He looked like he was going to say something but shook his head instead. She pulled her hand away and he let it go, but neither one of them took a step back. It seemed every time this happened, it got harder to move away. How long would it be this way? When would it settle back down?

Could it settle? The questions unnerved her because the answers weren't simple.

A crash in the hallway, followed by a much-too-close laugh, sent Maggie hopping backward, shaking her head to clear the cobwebs from her brain. Where did her brain go when she got close to Josh? They were in a public place with the door half-open. People were drawing quick, gleeful conclusions as it was.

She needed to get out of here pronto. "Well. I'm sure we've taken up enough of your time. I just wanted to make sure you had your lunch. I'll, um, go get Cody and get him out of Teresa's hair."

He cleared his throat. "Yeah. I'll be up there in a second."

Maggie made her escape and slipped through the confusion of hallways—why did all doctor's offices seem to be laid out in an indecipherable way?—and finally found Cody on an extra chair next to Teresa. When he saw her he gave her a big grin and held up three suckers.

"Look, Maggie! These are for later," he explained and Teresa sent him a fond look.

"You have to ask first, remember," she reminded him. "Are you on your way out?" she asked Maggie.

"In a minute. I think Josh is coming up here to say bye to Cody." So she was trapped here a little longer.

"Josh is a good man," Teresa said, not quite casually.

Uh-oh. "Yes, he is," Maggie replied. Could the floor please open up now and swallow her before this went any further?

Teresa tipped her head toward Cody, who was showing his windfall to another nurse. "He needs a good woman. So does Cody."

Maggie's cheeks grew hot and she resisted the urge to

run. "Of course they do. I'm sure he'll find someone perfect." The words jammed up in her throat.

Teresa eyed her for a moment. "Well, it was real nice to meet you," she said. "Come back and visit us, okay? We all love to see Cody."

"I'm sure they will," Josh said from somewhere behind her and Maggie's traitorous pulse flared. She hoped Teresa didn't notice her pink face and ask any questions.

What would she say?

Later that afternoon, Maggie put away the lunch dishes. Cody was coloring at the table. "Hey, Code. It's almost time for your swimming lesson."

"Oh, yeah!" Cody abandoned the crayons and ran upstairs, presumably in search of his bathing suit and towel. The lessons had been her idea, something that got him out of the house for a little bit and interacting with other kids. In the winter he'd start preschool.

It was a short drive to the local YMCA. Cody changed quickly in a family locker room and they walked through to the pool area together. There were ten other kids there, and the instructor was a young man who couldn't be that far out of high school. Cody walked to the pool and Maggie sat in one of the plastic chairs that lined the pool area. The other parents—mostly moms, but there were one or two dads—were chatting among themselves. She reached into her bag for the novel she'd brought along.

"You're with Cody Tanner?" A male voice, deep, pleasant. She glanced up to see a handsome man sitting next to her, probably a few years younger. She gave him a quick smile. "I am. I'm his nanny. Maggie Thelan."

He nodded and offered his hand. "Jake Curtis." His shake was firm and warm but there weren't any of the sparks she got from Josh. "I'm Ellie's dad. In the pink flower suit."

The little blond girl was talking to Cody and he was chattering back. "They seem to be friends," Maggie noted.

Jake nodded. "They do. This is my first week. My ex usually brings her."

Maggie recognized the subtle way of letting her know he was single. It flustered her a bit and she fumbled with her bookmark. She wasn't used to this. "Ah. Well. I may have seen her last week, then."

"Maybe." He stretched out his long legs, and Maggie thought it really was a shame she couldn't find enough chemistry to pursue this. Maybe it would come in time? Was it worth it, to take her mind off Josh? She didn't want to use Jake, even if he was willing.

Jake was funny and warm and friendly. He didn't come on too strong but was clear in his interest. At the end of the half-hour lesson he had her laughing and she was much more at ease. But she didn't feel anything other than friendliness.

He looked at her with a direct gaze. "If I asked you out, Maggie, would you go?"

She swallowed hard. "Oh, Jake."

"We just met. I know. I'm not asking for much, just the chance to talk more over coffee or something."

Maggie put her book back into her bag, her mind whirling. "I can't promise it will go anywhere," she said finally. "But I'd love to have coffee with a friend."

He held her gaze and nodded. "That's fine with me. Are you free tonight?"

She was, as it happened. They set a time and a place. He offered to pick her up, but she declined. It seemed wrong somehow, making it more than it was. Plus…she'd feel she had to justify it to Josh.

She gathered Cody, got him dressed and hurried out to the car, one thought running on a loop though her brain.

What would Josh say?

Worse, why did it matter?

Chapter Six

"Do you need me tonight?" Maggie asked Josh when he got home.

He pulled off his gloves. "No. We should be good. You have plans?"

Her split-second hesitation caused his antenna to go on alert. She wouldn't quite meet his eyes. "I do. Yes. I'm meeting a friend for coffee."

"A friend," Josh repeated. He didn't want to ask but he would bet this friend was male. His stomach soured.

"The father of one of Cody's friends from swimming," she said.

He went very still. "I see." He heard the stiffness in his tone and tried to soften it. "Well. Your time is your own, of course."

She still wouldn't look at him. "Yes, it is. I won't be late."

"You've got a key," Josh said tightly. Damn it, why did it matter? He didn't want anything to happen. She was looking elsewhere. Wasn't that what he wanted?

Still, this unfamiliar feeling could only be jealousy. It'd been so many years since he'd experienced it and it didn't feel any better now that he was older and supposedly wiser. "Can I ask who?" *So I can go hurt him later?* The vehemence of the thought made him wince.

"Jake Curtis. Do you know him?"

The hell of it was, he did and liked the guy. "I do. He's a good guy." The truth was sand in his mouth.

She reached for her coat and slipped her arms in the sleeves, finally meeting his eyes. In hers was a plea for understanding. "This isn't a date, Josh. There's no danger of me putting something like this in front of my job."

"I'm not worried about that." He saw the flash in her eyes and realized he sounded dismissive. "I'm not worried you'll be less than professional with us," he amended awkwardly.

"Well, then," she said, her posture stiff. "I'll be on my way. See you later."

He made one attempt to be a bigger person as she grabbed her purse. "Have fun," he managed to say past the dryness in his throat. She looked at him oddly and he knew he wasn't fooling her.

"Do you know something about him I need to be aware of?" she asked, concern in her voice.

Josh sighed. "No. Like I said, Jake's a good man." The admission was grudging but not because it wasn't true— but because it *was* true. Jake was a good guy, much better than himself. Quite possibly without the emotional ball and chain Josh hauled around.

"All right." Maggie turned toward the door. "I'll be back in a bit."

"Okay." Josh forced himself not to walk to the front window and watch her leave. To meet another man. He ground his teeth together but had to smile when Cody came in the room and gave him a hug. "Hey, big guy. How was your day?"

Cody filled him in, and Josh did his best to put Maggie out of his mind. It wasn't any of his business what she did. He needed to act like it. He couldn't have her.

He knew this. So it wasn't fair to her for him to get all possessive.

But it didn't make him feel any better.

Ten minutes later, his phone rang. He answered without even looking at the display. Part of him hoped it was Maggie. *Stupid.*

"So, Josh. Does Maggie have plans for Thanksgiving?" His mother's voice bubbled through the phone.

She might now. The thought was unwelcome and unbidden. She was out with Jake, for God's sake. Anything was possible. He cleared his throat. This would be a tricky conversation. "Well. I don't know. I can ask her."

"Can you ask her now? I'm looking at a turkey right now."

"Um. Well, no. She's out." Josh really didn't want to have to say it.

"Oh, okay. I'll just call her cell. Thanks—"

"No! No, Mom, that's not necessary. I'll ask her when she gets home." Right there was his mistake. He shut his eyes and waited.

She didn't disappoint. "Joshua Tanner, what aren't you telling me?"

Bingo. He opened his eyes and stared into the flames in the fireplace. "She's out for coffee with a friend. There's nothing to tell. It's just rude to interrupt her." It was true. That and Cody were the only things keeping him from going after her right now. Why did he care?

"A friend," Ellen repeated slowly, her displeasure clear in her tone. "Is she on a date?"

He heard the accusation in her voice and let his head fall back on the couch. "It's not a date, Mom." So Maggie had said, several times. Who was she trying to convince? Him or herself?

"You let her go out with another man?" Ellen's voice spiked with incredulity. "Are you an idiot?"

In spite of himself, Josh choked out a laugh. "Mom. Jeez. How does that make me an idiot? She's a young woman. Single." Gorgeous. Sweet. Sexy. *Not helping.* "She can date if she wants." Hell if the thought didn't make his gut even more sour. A completely useless reaction since he had no claim on her or her time.

A pause. "Josh—"

"Mom, don't start," he interrupted. "Please. I'm not dating. No reason she can't." If he said it enough would he finally believe it?

"Oh, Josh." Tenderness and frustration mixed in her voice. "How can you not see what's right under your nose? How can you just let her walk out of your life like that?"

"Easy," Josh lied. "She's the nanny. Not my girlfriend."

"And that's a damn shame," Ellen muttered. She sighed. "I know, I know, I need to butt out. It's your life. But it's so hard to see you've got a shot at happiness. I like Maggie, Josh. She's such a great girl. But you're letting her slip right by you."

Josh gritted his teeth. "I'm not letting anything go, Mom. There'd have to be something to let go and there's not. So I'll ask her about Thanksgiving when she gets back, okay?"

A long pause. Then she said, "Okay. I'll wait on the turkey. But let me know soon."

Josh promised he would and hung up before she started in on another polite lecture on how he should move on. Damn it, in theory he knew that. If things were different, if Lucy hadn't died, if they'd simply divorced, maybe then he could see himself pursuing Maggie. Maybe. As it was, life hadn't gone that way for him. Certainly it hadn't for Lucy.

He'd do well to remember that.

Headlights washed over the wall as a car turned into the driveway. He glanced at his watch. Maggie. He refused to examine why he felt a flood of relief. She hadn't been gone long, just over an hour.

It'd been a long damn hour.

Back at home—and it was home to Maggie now—she put the car in Park. Cody's window was dark. He'd probably just gone to bed. She got out of the car, surprised at how hesitant she felt about seeing Josh. *If he meant nothing to you it wouldn't matter.* The truth of that slipped under her heart and settled in. She tried to ignore it as she walked to the door.

She let herself in and saw him in the living room. Her breath caught. Even in pajama pants and a faded Michigan State sweatshirt he was flat-out sexy.

He stood up and came over to lean on the doorway. "How was your evening?"

"Fine." She slipped off her boots and put them in the closet before turning to face him fully. She needed to set this straight, for her own sake. "It wasn't a date, Josh. I'm not looking for anything." *But if I were, you'd be it.* The thought set her reeling and she pushed it away. "I don't want you to think I'd put something like dating before Cody. My responsibility lies with him."

He didn't move. "That's good to hear. But Maggie, I don't expect you to give up your life for us."

She laughed a little. What life? "I don't look at it that way." It wasn't a sacrifice. She loved Cody and this job.

He looked at her steadily. "That's good to know." He paused. "Do you have a minute?"

"Sure." She followed him in the living room and perched across from him on a chair, nerves on alert.

"What are you doing for Thanksgiving?"

The question threw her. "Oh." She paused, then smoothed her hands on her jeans. This was a conversation she'd like to avoid. "I'm not sure yet. I might join my friend Kerry, I guess."

"Not your family?"

The simple question would have brought her to her knees if she'd been standing. "Um, no. My mother and I are estranged. My father is…gone."

He looked stricken, like he'd stepped in it. "I'm sorry," he murmured.

She shrugged, the gesture casual though she felt anything but. "It is what it is." She couldn't keep the note of sorrow from her tone.

"Will you join us?" His voice was soft.

Her head snapped up. She hadn't expected that. "You?"

"And Cody and my mom. Or did—did Jake invite you?" The last was spoken stiffly.

She sputtered a laugh. "I just met him and I'm not interested in him in that way. So no. He didn't. But I don't want to intrude on your holiday. Thanksgiving is about family." The irony of her words wasn't lost on her. "Really, that's very kind—"

"Please, Maggie." The intensity of his gaze unsettled her. "Cody would love to have you."

She barked out a little laugh. "Playing the kid card, huh?"

Now humor glinted in those whiskey eyes. "Did it work?"

"I don't know, Josh. I'm not sure it's a good idea." She could tell him why, should tell him why, but couldn't get the words to form.

"Please."

The word was quiet and simple and oh, she was such a sucker for his voice. Her throat closed up. "I'll let you know tomorrow," she managed to respond after a moment and stood up. It was time to go to upstairs before she got pulled any further in.

"Fair enough."

She bade him good-night and escaped, afraid if she looked back, she'd see him watching her.

In the safety of her room, Maggie flipped the switch on her fireplace, then pulled out her phone.

Before she could accept Josh's invitation, she needed to see what her mom was planning. While they hadn't spoken in weeks and Linda had been very clear in her stance on Maggie's quest to learn about Lucy, she couldn't risk Linda's being alone on Thanksgiving. No doubt she'd get shot down but she had to try.

Since the conversation with her mother would be ugly, she dawdled. First a shower. Then the call. She dropped the phone on her bed and padded into the bathroom to start the shower. Josh's invitation to Thanksgiving caught her off guard. Ellen's doing or not, it was a family day. Those lines that held her sanity were getting thinner by the day. This whole situation had the ring of false intimacy. Meals together. Shared experiences about Cody. They even occasionally went places as a unit. None of it was real, even though they seemed to work well together—when the attraction was under control, of course.

Lately that seemed harder and harder. If only there'd been true sparks with Jake.

She stripped off her clothes and dropped them in the hamper. She pulled out the band that held her hair in its usual ponytail and ran her fingers through its heavy mass. A wry smile touched her lips. Stick-straight, no matter what she did to it. She'd learned to accept it, but through adolescence it had been the bane of her existence.

She could see herself, naked, in the misty mirror. Long and thin, a bit of a waist. A few curves, but nothing that could be considered lush. Medium-sized breasts, full and heavy, still firm. The dark wash of her hair fell over her shoulders and the ends brushed her nipples.

With a sigh, she turned from the mirror and stepped in the shower. Tony had always said she was too tall, too thin. No curves. Not womanly enough. Now that she thought about it, what had she ever seen in him? Why had she put up with it for so long?

No easy answer there.

Of course, he'd never looked at her like Josh sometimes did. Like something to be desired, to be wanted. Like she was beautiful. Despite the hot water, goose bumps rose on her skin just thinking about it.

She pressed her hands to her eyes. Okay, okay, this was wrong on so many levels, to be in her dead half sister's house, fantasizing about her dead half sister's husband. There were no two ways about it. She reached for her scrubby and soap and rubbed her skin as if she could peel the thoughts of Josh right off her, down the drain.

You can't have him, Maggie. Even if you weren't the nanny, you can't have him. The little voice wasn't taunting, just matter-of-fact. She tilted her face to the spray, let it wash the unexpected tears away. Figured. One decent man, and she couldn't have him. Worse, she couldn't even find the words to tell him why she couldn't have him. The risk of losing Cody was too great.

She stayed in the shower until she felt she had herself back under control, then stepped out and yanked a towel off the rack. Drying quickly, she pulled on a T-shirt and flannel pj bottoms—plaid, not the goofy prints Josh seemed to prefer—toweled her hair and padded out into the bedroom where the fire crackled. Oh, how she loved this space. Homey, warm and, frankly, if this was her house, it would be her bedroom anyway. It was a sanctuary.

She flipped open her cell, took a deep breath and hit her mom's speed-dial number. When it rang and rang she held her breath. It'd be best to get this conversation over with. But if she had to leave a message—

"Maggie." Her mother's cool voice filled her ear. Maggie's insides lurched at the unfriendliness in her mother's tone.

"Hi, Mom." Shaking slightly, she sank in a chair. "How are you?"

A pause. "How do you think I am? My husband betrayed me. My daughter, too. How should I be, Maggie?"

The bitterness in the words hit Maggie in the heart. So this was how it would be. She'd expected it, but still. "Mom. I didn't—"

"You did." Her mother's voice was deceptively quiet. "Oh, yes, you did. I thought I could count on you. But you chose *him*." She spat the last word.

Maggie stared at the fire, grief twisting in her heart. It wasn't that way, had never been. Finding Lucy had been something she was driven to do. A piece of her that she hadn't even known she'd been missing—but once she'd realized, she'd needed to fill the void. Clearly, her mother didn't see it that way. "I don't know what to say, Mom."

"Do they know who you are, Maggie?" Linda's words were hard. "Did you tell them?"

She drew in a deep breath. "No. Not yet. I will."

"And what will happen then? They'll get rid of you. You'll have nothing. *Nothing*. Like me. You don't know what I've been through." The bitterness wound like poison through her words.

Maggie's eyes watered. Okay then. "I'm sorry, Mom. I really am. I—"

Linda cut her off. "I don't want your apology. When you've come to your senses and let this go, call me. Not a minute before."

Click. The dead air rang in her ear.

Maggie stared at the fire through the tears burning her eyes. The firelight made little shadows and patterns on the walls.

Shadows and light. Like the little pockets of life where people hid their secrets, hoping they wouldn't come out to see the light of day.

Of course, some of those secrets were a bit bigger than others.

Like the one her father had kept for thirty-something years, from those who loved him the most. And the one she now held, the fruit of that original secret. She didn't know why her father had kept it for so long, only that he'd honored the request of the mother.

But not why he'd honored it. Was that what ate at her mother now, that maybe he'd loved another woman enough to keep her secret for over three decades?

Resolved, she yanked open her door and went back downstairs. She hadn't even asked her mother the question but had clearly gotten the answer.

Josh was still in the living room. When she walked in, he half turned, surprise on his face.

"I'll come." Did her voice just tremble?

He blinked at her. "Okay."

"Thanksgiving," she clarified. "Thank you for the invite." She turned to go upstairs before she made a fool of herself when the tears came.

He stood up quickly, came around the chair and caught her hand. "You're welcome. Maggie. Um. You look— Are you all right?"

His concern caused tears to burn in her throat. "Of

course." Other than being rejected by her mother. Again. When would she learn? Would she ever learn?

"You're going to cry," he said softly and there was an undertone of horror that would have made her laugh under different circumstances.

She shook her head and the traitorous tears clung to her lashes. "No. I'm. Not." Spoken through gritted teeth. She'd hold it together until she got back to her room.

Josh couldn't help it. Those big blue eyes shimmering with tears simply did him in. He touched her face, the warm satin of her skin. Smelled the fresh, fruity scent of shampoo from her still-damp hair. Heard her sharp intake of breath as her hand came up to rest on his chest, but she didn't pull away. His gaze locked on her blue one, and he saw his own desire reflected in hers. The wanting twined around them, silky, sweet and hot.

Dangerous.

His gaze dipped to her mouth and it nearly killed him when her tongue slid across her lower lip. He moved closer, the heat of her body mingling with his. If she tipped her head a little to the right and he moved a little to the left he could finally taste her. Steal the kiss he craved, so much so she'd been haunting his dreams, his waking hours. God, how he wanted to kiss her, to wrap himself in her. He hadn't been this close to a woman in—

Years.

Hell. *Lucy.*

Something must have shown on his face because she stepped back quickly, so much so she stumbled and nearly ended up on her backside on the couch.

"Um. Yeah. This is so not a good idea," she said, the words coming out in a rush. "I'm your employee, and your—" She stopped. Something flashed over her face, so fast he almost didn't catch it but it looked a lot like guilt.

Not half of what he felt right now, no doubt.

"My what?"

She shook her head. "Listen. In my marriage I got involved with my boss. I *married* my boss, I mean. When it ended—very badly—I realized what a stupid mistake I'd made. Not that we'll get married." She waved her hands, then clamped them over her eyes, her face turning a pink he found disturbingly adorable. "I don't mean that. I mean I can't risk my job. Plus, there's Cody—" Her voice trailed off as she wrapped her arms around her middle and looked at him beseechingly.

He stepped back. Her point was clear. It shook him to his core, how badly he wanted her. He cleared his throat. "You're right, of course. Though your job is safe, Maggie. Always." He shoved his hands in his pockets so he didn't reach for her again, mistake or not, and brought the conversation back to safer topics, as if he hadn't almost kissed her. "So. Okay. Thanksgiving. I'll let my mom know."

Sorrow crossed her face. "You are so lucky to have a mom like Ellen." The wistfulness in her tone hit him.

Matchmaking aside, of course. "I know." He left it at that. Her wrecked expression made sense now. She'd probably gone to call her estranged mother, made a stab at spending the holiday together.

And he'd nearly kissed her. What kind of guy was he?

She didn't meet his gaze as she turned to leave. "Well. Okay then. Good night, Josh."

He watched her escape, helpless. He'd very nearly crossed a line tonight, one he'd drawn himself and fiercely guarded. Not just crossed it, but left it in the dust. Every day he slipped a little farther into territory he was in no way ready for and the woman he wanted to share it with made it clear she wasn't, either, and would probably never be.

He rubbed his hand over his face, frustration a hard knot in his stomach. Why the hell couldn't he get this back under control?

Chapter Seven

Marta looked at him over her glasses the next morning, her dark eyes shrewd. "So. Who was the woman in the window last night?"

Josh blinked. He'd barely had any sleep, between hot dreams starring the nanny and his mind replaying how close he'd come to kissing her. Now Marta wanted to tell him riddles? "What woman? What window?"

Marta reached over and whacked him lightly on the arm with the chart she'd been writing in. "Your woman. Your window."

"My—" Josh started, then stopped. He had a feeling he wasn't going to like this. "What are you talking about?"

Marta glanced at her watch. "I got a call last night about eight-thirty from Betty Martin, who happened to be driving home from bingo night at the American Legion and passing your house when she chanced to look over and see you and a dark-haired woman in a passionate embrace in front of the window." Marta lifted an eyebrow, her expression almost gleeful.

I wish. The unbidden thought nearly derailed his train of thought. "We all know Mrs. Martin needs her glasses updated. I'm not even sure why she's still driving," Josh hedged, hoping to divert the conversation, but Marta shook her head. He sighed, gave in. "She's mistaken. Maggie and I were talking in the living room. Mrs. Martin must have seen us standing there." Clearly, she'd taken some pretty big leaps from what should have been a glimpse. Next time he'd make sure the drapes were closed. Just in case. *There will be no next time.*

Marta studied him for a moment, long enough that Josh wanted to squirm. The she sighed. "That's too bad. We all know you need a woman in your life."

Not again. "Marta. I'm not—" he began but she cut him off with a wave of her hand.

"I know you're not. Not one like Julie Henney. I like Maggie. There's nothing between you?"

Josh shook his head. "Of course not. She's Cody's nanny, for God's sake." Oh, listen to him now. He'd very nearly kissed her last night, and no doubt would if given the chance again, despite everything. What a hypocrite he was.

Marta harrumphed. "Like that matters."

"You'd be surprised." It mattered to Maggie. He'd respect that. No matter how enticing her mouth was. Too bad he couldn't ask Marta what the hell he was doing to give himself away. At this point, denying he found Maggie attractive was pointless.

Her cell phone rang then, saving him from answering. He shrugged and, as she walked away, she sent him a look he knew meant she wasn't finished.

Marta could wish all she wanted. He knew she wanted him happy, the way she and Trav were. He understood that and appreciated it. But in the end, it was up to him and Maggie. She'd been clear on her boundaries. God knew he had his own, even if he'd been getting his priorities screwed up lately. There were far too many things stacked against them.

Which was fine. If they dated and things went bad— and they would, he had no doubt—what happened then?

He'd proven once before he wasn't relationship material. What would they do then?

He couldn't afford to lose her. She was wonderful with his son and Cody depended on her. So did he. Their lives were so much smoother since he'd hired her. Fuller, too. They felt like a family. While he knew it should be wrong, it didn't feel that way.

It felt…right.

But it shouldn't. What about what he'd promised Lucy?

As he tried to shove the thoughts away and concentrate on getting ready for the patients of the day, he couldn't shake one funny little thought.

Despite all the reasons why not, he was determined to kiss Maggie.

The next morning, Maggie sat on the floor of Cody's bedroom, playing with Matchbox cars and doing her best not to think about Josh and what had almost transpired between them last night. Her body heated when she thought of the intensity in his gaze and how much she'd wanted him to kiss her, no matter how bad an idea it was.

A good dash of reality was how quickly he'd backed off. Lucy's ghost had intervened on both their ends. Just as well. She tamped down the regret. No use going there, though it wasn't lost on her she was obsessing about the kiss she couldn't have—and had missed twice—with Josh rather than the one she could have had with Jake.

She wouldn't make that mistake again. Until she and Josh dealt with this thing growing between them, she'd be more careful.

Cody zoomed a truck with extra zeal and it careened across the hardwood floor and under the bed.

"Uh-oh," Maggie said, ashamed she'd let her focus drift so far off track. "Can you reach it?"

A pause. "Aw, I can't get it." Cody's voice was muffled as he rooted around under the bed. "I can't get it, Maggie."

"Here, let me try." She kneeled down as he scooted out and sat back. She looked under the bed and almost laughed. "Goodness, Code, is this where you store everything when you clean your room?"

"Sometimes," he admitted without a trace of apology.

Maggie bit back a grin. Of course, it was easier to shove stuff under the bed when you were four. Now that she was onto him, she'd help him clean under here next time.

"Okay." She squinted under the bed and saw the truck, resting against…a photo album? Her heart began to jump as she pulled both items out. Trying to keep her voice and hands steady, she held out the leather-bound book. "What's this, Cody?"

He brightened and reached for it. "My Mama book. I don't have a mama anymore. But Daddy and Gramma made me this book so I'd 'member her."

Maggie's throat burned with tears. "Oh, Cody." What else was there to say? "Will you share it with me?"

Fire truck forgotten, he settled next to her on the floor and opened the album. On the first page was a picture of a woman with dark curly hair, cut short. Her shining blue eyes were the same shade as Cody's, almost as Maggie's own. She had the same nose as their father. She held a tiny baby and smiled widely into the camera. Even dressed in a faded hospital gown and with no makeup, she was gorgeous.

Maggie swallowed hard. *Lucy.* The half sister she'd never known. Finally, she had a beautiful face to put with the name. She touched the page with a trembling hand.

"That's me," Cody said. "I just got borned. She's so pretty."

Afraid the tears gathering in her eyes would fall on the

pages of the precious Mama book, Maggie shifted position slightly. "She sure is," she agreed, her voice a rasp in her throat.

"Daddy says she can't come back 'cause she got dead," he said matter-of-factly as he turned the page. Maggie's heart ripped at the words.

"She loved you very much," Maggie said, because the truth was on these pages, in these images. In every one, Lucy looked at her baby boy and radiated joy, love and pride. A vibrant beauty, she looked to have embraced motherhood with gusto. Maggie couldn't take her eyes off the pictures. Something about them fed her soul, helped to heal the hole learning of Lucy's death had left.

Cody didn't look at her. "Then why did she leave?"

Maggie slid her arm around the little boy's shoulders and pulled him against her, not able to stop the flow of tears now. His question had no real answer but she gave it her best shot. "She didn't leave you on purpose. I'm sure your dad has told you that. She'd never have left you on purpose." The truth of that shone from this album. Clearly both Josh and Lucy loved their son.

"I miss her." The wistfulness in Cody's voice was wrenching. No doubt he didn't remember Lucy, since he'd been barely a year when she'd died, but he knew enough to know his mom should be here.

"I know." Maggie missed her dad fiercely.

"Maybe someday I can have a new mom," Cody said with the resilience typical of little kids.

"Mmm," Maggie said noncommittally. This was a conversation she and Cody could not have.

"You can be my new mom," Cody suggested, and Maggie sucked in a breath at the hopeful look on his face. "You look kinda like my mama and my daddy likes you. *I* like you."

Oh, no. She gave his shoulders a little squeeze and tried to keep her voice steady. "Well, Cody, I'm very honored but it's not that easy. I like you and your dad very much. But it's not like picking out a new puppy," she said carefully. The potential minefields of this conversation weren't hers to navigate. Josh needed to talk to him. "But I'm here as your nanny and I'm not going anywhere." She smiled, hoping he'd let it go.

He looked pensive for a moment, then glanced up at the window. He scrambled up. "Look, Maggie! It's snowing!"

Grateful for the change in subject, she placed the book on his nightstand as she peered out the window. The white stuff fell steadily, already making a light blanket on the ground. "Well, look at that. Do you want to go outside?"

Cody's whoop carried back into the room as he ran out into the hall. She grinned through the dampness in her eyes. "I take it that's a yes." She lingered for a second, her hand on the cover of the photo album. "Hi, Lucy," she said softly. "You've got an amazing family."

Then she wiped away the tears and went downstairs.

Maggie surveyed the damage on the back of Cody's winter coat with dismay and amusement. The fact the snow hadn't really stuck to the ground hadn't deterred him from attempting a snow angel—maybe dirt angel was a better term—and the coat now sported serious grass stains. She sprayed it with stain remover and stuffed it in the washer. Then, as it had all day, it hit her she'd finally seen a picture of Lucy.

She shut her eyes for a moment against the little stab of pain. If she kept her sister's face front and center, she'd be able to keep her feelings for Josh at bay. As it should be. She could make peace with that. Someday.

When she turned around, she gave a little shriek. Josh

stood there, looking as startled as she was. Her face started to heat and she wondered if she looked as guilty as she felt.

"Sorry," he said, a small grin playing around the corners of his mouth. She forced herself to look away. "I thought you heard me."

"No, I was just…thinking about grass stains," she blurted.

He arched an eyebrow.

"Cody's snow angels from today," she explained. "There wasn't enough snow for it. So, grass stains. On everything."

The smile was full-blown now and her breath caught. "That's my boy," he said, and she couldn't help but smile with him.

"So. Did you need something?" She turned to the load of Cody's things she'd removed from the dryer. Anything to keep her hands busy.

He sobered. "No. Not really." He thrust his hands in his pockets and she realized he was nervous. "I just wanted to make sure we're still on track even after last night."

She lowered her eyes to the shirt she held. Last night and the time in the truck a few weeks ago. The shame rose sharply in her throat. "Of course. We're adults, right?"

"Right." He cleared his throat. "Listen, about Jake—"

She cut him off. "There's no Jake. I mean, there's no relationship potential there. He might be another friend, but that's all. I wouldn't have come home from a real date and, well, almost kiss you."

There it was. To say it was to own it and now that she'd put it out there it was too late to take it back. Her cheeks flamed and she could not look at him, couldn't risk the eye contact and what she'd see there. *Why couldn't he just have let it go?*

"Maggie." He touched her arm gently and she forced

herself to look up. His gaze was shuttered. "I know that." He paused and a muscle in his jaw ticked. "I just wanted you to know if you wanted to date him—or anyone— while of course you don't need my permission, there'd be no problem with your job."

Oh, well, of course. Right.

"Good to know." She reached for another item of clothing. What did she want him to say? He wanted her, wanted a relationship with her? She'd have to turn him down. She'd been clear on her lines last night. Today, they'd been cemented when she'd seen Lucy's face. Since there was nowhere else for this conversation to go, she said, with a calmness she didn't feel, "Anything else?"

He stood there for a moment, then shook his head. "No. Nothing else."

She let him leave, holding her breath as she listened to him go upstairs. When she heard his footsteps overhead she released the breath with a sharp gust and leaned her head on her hand, tears of frustration stinging her eyes. The right woman would make him realize his promise only hurt himself and Cody. Cody needed a mom. Not to replace Lucy, never that, but to help fill the void her death left behind.

She knew she wasn't that woman. She couldn't give him what he'd need. She'd been unable to do it in her first marriage. Why would this time be different?

As she started up the stairs, a thought hit her and rocked her to her toes.

What on earth would she do when he met the right woman?

Maggie checked her list one last time. Being the day before Thanksgiving, she had a pie to bake—her contribution to the dinner. The grocery store would be a zoo, so she wanted to get in and out as early as possible. Pulling on her coat, she headed for her car. She tossed her purse on the seat and turned the ignition.

Bangbangbangbangbang.

Startled, she shut the car off. That didn't sound good. Maybe it was just cold? She tried again.

Bangbangbangbangbang.

Well, crap. She snatched the key out with a frown and looked up to see Josh crossing toward her. He hadn't grabbed a jacket.

"What the hell was that?" he asked.

"I, um, have no idea." She slid out and stared at her car with a frown. "It sounds bad."

He gave a half laugh and inclined his head. "Yeah. Pop the hood. Let's take a look."

She did and he lifted it up, stared inside. She came around to stand beside him. He smelled so good, a little woodsy and spicy. She tried not to take a deep sniff. Tried not to picture him almost kissing her. And failed on both counts.

"I'm no mechanic, but I'm guessing that's your problem." He pointed to what even she could see was a broken belt.

"Oh, no." Her poor car. She shoved her hands in her pockets. "How does that happen? How do I fix it?" And goodness, how expensive was it to fix?

Josh already had his phone out. "I can call Trav. He's a great mechanic. That okay with you?"

She hesitated for a heartbeat. "Of course. I… Thank you." She didn't want to owe him anything, but clearly at this point she was stuck.

He dialed and had a brief conversation, then disconnected. "He's on his way. Why don't you take my car? Get what you need at the store."

"Oh." It was tempting, given how much work she had to do. "Are you sure?"

"Of course. Here. Give me your keys. I'll get mine for you." She dropped her keys in his hand, careful not to touch him, even with her gloves. He walked back inside while she retrieved her purse and list from her poor broken car.

In the garage, he handed over his keys. "Trav will take good care of your car. And he won't do anything until you okay it."

"That's good. I trust you." Her gaze locked on his as she said the words and she realized she meant them in a way far beyond fixing her car. *Oh, no.* Her breath caught in her throat as her color rose. Hoping he hadn't noticed, she broke eye contact and hopped in the SUV. With shaking hands she started it—no bad noises—and backed out. He stood off to the side and watched.

The fact the interior smelled like Josh wasn't helping her nerves settle. She closed her hands around the steering wheel and drove down the street, her own words ringing in her head. *I trust you.* How could she trust him? Why Josh? Was it because he was off-limits to her and therefore somehow safe?

Then she nearly laughed. Who was she kidding? Josh wasn't safe. He made her feel and want dangerous things that she had no business feeling or wanting. None at all, and most certainly not with him.

So far, her heart wasn't getting the message.

Trav stared down at the mess in the engine. "You weren't kidding."

"Nope." Josh had dressed for the cold this time and he stood next to his friend as he examined the crippled car. "You want it in the garage?"

It took a few minutes but they pushed the Impala into the still-cold garage but were at least spared the wind and snow. Trav opened the hood again.

"Made a hell of a noise," Josh observed. "I heard it all the way in the house."

Trav laughed. "I bet. Okay. I brought a bunch of belts actually. Let me see what I've got that will fit."

Trav was halfway done when Maggie pulled back in.

She walked up, shopping bag and two cups of to-go coffee in hand. "Hi, Trav. Thanks for doing this." She set the bag down and offered the coffee. "I thought you guys could use this."

As he took the cup, he sent her a warm smile that would have curdled Josh's insides if his best friend hadn't been happily married. "Thanks. And no problem. You had a bit of a surprise when you tried to start this, huh?"

"Ah. Well." She gave a little laugh. "A little." She paused. "You'll send me a bill?"

Trav shook his head. "I had the belt and the time. It's on me, Maggie."

She started to shake her head but he cut her off. "It's my pleasure."

"Well." She chewed on her lower lip and Josh's gaze zeroed right in on that lush lip. What he wouldn't give to have her nip at his own. He blinked, trying to shake the thought and unwanted surge of heat.

"Thank you," she said to Trav, and he nodded.

She turned to Josh and held out the second cup. He took it. "Thanks. It's cold out here."

She stood and chatted with Trav for a few minutes longer and Josh tried not to look at her. It was so damn hard. She drew him like the proverbial moth to a flame—only they were both likely to get burned. *I trust you.*

He was starting to think she shouldn't.

"Well, I've got to get started on this pie," she said brightly. "Let me know when you're done."

"Will do," Trav said.

Josh stepped closer as she turned to walk away and tucked a loose strand of hair over her shoulder. He knew it was a dumb move but he just couldn't help it. "Did you get what you needed?"

Her gaze flew to his. He could see the pulse jumping at her throat. She wasn't any more immune to him than he was to her. The thought both aroused and scared him.

"I did. Thanks." She pulled his keys out of her pocket and held them out with a slightly shaking hand. "Here."

He took them with his free hand, letting his fingers graze hers. Her eyes widened slightly at the contact and she moved toward the door.

When he turned back around, Trav's knowing gaze was on him. "Josh?"

There was a world of admonition in the word. He knew what Trav wasn't saying. "Yeah."

"You want to tell me what the hell you're doing?"

Josh examined the car engine, not really seeing it. Talk about a loaded question. Not one he could answer, either. "Not really."

"Can't stay away, can you?"

Josh sipped his coffee, deliberately avoiding the question. "She lives here."

"Not what I meant."

His grip tightened on the cup. "What do you want me to say, Trav? We've been over this. It's not gonna happen. End of story."

"Chicken."

Josh nearly choked. "Excuse me?"

Trav looked at him steadily. "You heard me. You're hiding behind Lucy. Behind what a mess your marriage was. Don't," he said when Josh started to object. "Think about it. Let's get this done before we freeze our asses off."

Shaken, Josh stared at the back of his friend's head. Trav wasn't right, couldn't be. He'd made a promise. That wasn't hiding.

Was it?

Chapter Eight

Thanksgiving morning, Maggie helped drag plastic storage totes full of Christmas lights out of the garage. Today was the Tanner family's traditional decorating day for Holden's Crossing's Light Parade the Saturday after Thanksgiving. She'd volunteered to help. Josh had explained all the houses on their street participated.

The wind was cold and there was a bit of snow spitting from the sky, but Josh didn't seem to notice as he strode around gathering extension cords and other items. It took a great deal of effort on Maggie's part not to watch him.

She forced herself to focus on the half dozen or so of the large plastic bins. When she popped them open, she could see they were packed full of light strings. On every bin was a laminated sheet describing where the contents went. Clearly, this was serious business.

"You do the whole house?" Maggie called when Josh walked back into the garage. She eyed the yard with its numerous trees and bushes and shrubs, then the two-story house. "Today? Before dinner?"

Josh set the ladder he'd been carrying down on the driveway with a clank. "Most of it. You'll see. We've got it down pretty good after all these years." He reached over and tugged lightly on her sleeve. "And this year we've got you. An extra set of hands. Bonus."

"Okay." Some of her skepticism must have shown in her voice because he gave her an amused side glance.

"Trust me." His words were spoken lightly but they reverberated in her heart. Of course, he wasn't talking about anything other than hanging Christmas lights. It spoke volumes about her state of mind that she'd even wished otherwise.

"I'll take your word for it," she said, keeping her tone equally light. "Where do we start?"

Josh picked up the clipboard holding instruction sheets and gestured for her to come closer. She stepped up next to him and tried to ignore the flare of awareness. "Trav and I will start on the house. That takes some time because of all the peaks. You and Marta can start on the porch and shrubs. It seems like a lot but all the clips and hooks are in place and we'll be almost done by dinner. Those trees out front are the hardest because the branches are wrapped in lights. We might not get those done till tomorrow."

Standing this close to him, staring at the written instructions she wasn't seeing thanks to her brain shorting out at his proximity, she was close enough that their arms touched. She could feel his heat through her down jacket.

Actually, that was the heat he generated in her.

She looked up at him, tried to shut the unwelcome thoughts down. "You really enjoy this."

"I do." He set the clipboard down. "My mom is the one who did all this organizing. She loves the Light Parade. I do it mostly for her, and Cody, too, now."

Maggie's heart, already on the line, tipped a little further. A man who would go to all this trouble for his mom and son was a man worth loving.

The thought stopped her breath.

Not willing to examine it too closely, she cleared her throat. "I think that's wonderful. I can't wait to see it."

He looked straight into her eyes, and just like that she was helpless to move. Could he see her feelings? His gaze dropped to her mouth. Involuntarily, she ran her tongue over her lower lip and saw his eyes darken.

The front door banged open and Cody flew out. Maggie took a small step backward and Josh did the same. They needed to stop falling into these small moments of longing and want. She didn't know how to avoid them, unless she flat-out avoided Josh.

Not really an option when they lived in the same house.

Cody trotted over, carrying with him the scent of roasting turkey from the house. "Are they here yet?"

Josh laughed. "Code, do you see the car?"

The little boy peered around them and frowned. "No."

"Soon," Josh promised. "Were you helping Gramma?"

Ellen had arrived before dawn, bearing all the necessities for the dinner. She'd turned down Maggie's offer of help, explaining she had the whole thing down to a science. Maggie was inclined to believe her.

"Yeah," Cody said. "I stirred the stuffin'."

"Awesome," Maggie said with a smile. "I bet it will be yummy."

Right then, the car pulled in the driveway, and Cody's attention shifted. She stood back as the friends greeted each other.

"Morning, Maggie," Trav said as he came to stand beside her. "How's the car running?"

"Just fine," she said with a smile. She liked this man, with his friendly manner and warmth. "Thanks again for the help."

Trav waved her off. "Don't mention it. Glad it was a simple fix."

Marta stopped, carrying a basket. "Maggie, good to see you. Is my husband boring you with car talk?"

She gave a little laugh. "No."

"Good. I'll be back out in a minute. Honey, try to keep the kids off the ladders. JT wants to see the view from the roof." She gave Maggie a little smile and walked away.

"Kids," Trav muttered. "Where do they get their ideas?"

Maggie called the boys over. When they showed up, she opened the box marked "front" and pulled out some net lights. "You guys want to help me do the bushes? I could use the extra hands."

The little boys put plenty of enthusiasm into the task and held her full attention so she didn't keep looking to see what Josh was doing. She surreptitiously straightened their most recent bush while they tackled the next.

Marta joined them. "Oh, good! More helpers. Looking good, boys." They beamed at her praise and went back to work.

To Maggie, she said quietly, watching as they squabbled a bit over who had more of the net, "Did you know decorating for Christmas was a contact sport?"

Maggie sputtered a laugh. "So I'm learning."

When the boys finished, Marta sent them into the backyard to play. As Maggie turned to see them round the house, her attention flew up the ladder to Josh, who was replacing clips and hanging lights. She had a great view of his jean-clad rear. Even from the ground she could see how well the denim hugged his butt and thighs. She tore her gaze away when Marta spoke.

"What was that?" Embarrassed to be caught, and by someone who knew Josh as well as Marta did to boot, she met Marta's gaze with trepidation.

"Like the view?" she asked, humor sparkling in her dark eyes.

Maggie's face heated. No easy feat considering they

were standing outside in twenty-degree weather. "I imagine any woman would," she managed to say.

Marta shrugged as she turned to walk back to the lights. "Possibly. But you're not just any woman to him."

Maggie's heart gave a kick. "I'm not sure what that means," she said carefully.

"Just what I said," Marta said. "Let's get this porch done."

The conversation stayed away from heavy topics for the duration, for which Maggie was grateful. Ellen came out after a while with coffee. Both men came off the ladders and Maggie gratefully accepted a cup. "I didn't realize I was cold till right now."

Behind her, Josh gave a low chuckle. His body blocked the wind and made her feel an entirely different kind of heat. She longed to lean back into his solid warmth, the way Marta did with Trav.

She inched forward instead. No point in torturing herself.

The wind was cold and there was the snap of snow in the air. Josh eyed the clouds as he stepped around her to examine the sky.

"Think that will hold off?"

Trav snorted. "With our luck, probably not. Wouldn't be the first time. At least it won't be rain."

"All right. Break's over," Josh said, setting his empty cup on the porch floor. "Let's get this done."

When the men left, Maggie and Marta turned their attention to the rest of their task and moved to the smaller trees on the edge of the yard. Marta set the plastic bin down and pulled out a coil of lights and an extension cord. "These are the easier trees. They don't get wrapped the same way the ones closer to the street do. Just run a string through each one. We can get them done pretty quickly."

Maggie took a light string. "How long have you worked for Josh?" The question seemed safe enough, small talk between two people who were getting to know each other.

Marta climbed up the stepladder to reach the higher branches of the short tree. "Eight years. He hired me straight out of nursing school. We went to high school together before that. He actually introduced me to Trav."

"Before or after high school?"

Marta laughed. "After. We've been together ever since." She looked down and caught Maggie's eye. "You'd be good for him, you know."

"Ah. Well—" Just like that the conversation spun away from her. She fought to keep her eyes on the woman in front of her and not seek Josh out like she knew she'd been doing all day. "I'm the nanny. It's not a possibility." She knew Marta would see though her flimsy excuse in a heartbeat.

Marta tossed the last of the string over the top of the tree and climbed down the ladder. "No? That's too bad."

They started for the next tree, Maggie manning the ladder this time. From the ground Marta said quietly, "I think you're fooling yourself, Maggie."

Maggie bobbled the lights. "What?"

"It's none of my business. We don't know each other well. But I do know Josh pretty well. Even if I didn't, I'd have to be blind not to notice how the two of you keep looking at each other when you think no one's looking." She looked up at Maggie. "You have your reasons for not pursuing it. He has his own. I get that. That's your business. But you should acknowledge what's there."

Maggie kept her attention on the lights she was draping with now-shaking hands. She'd had no idea she was so transparent. "Well, that's a bit of a problem. I'm his employee, Marta. I can admit he's a very good-looking man—" complete understatement "—but I'm not up for a casual fling, much less a relationship, and I doubt he is, either. Plus Cody is in the house." *And I'm his sister-in-law.* The best reason of all.

Marta watched her come back down the ladder. "I don't think there's anything casual there," she said quietly. "But I'll let it go. I'm not trying to make you uncomfortable. I want the best for Josh. He deserves it more than anyone I know. And I tend to meddle a bit," she admitted. "Trav told me not to but I can't help it. Josh is like a brother to me. I'm sorry."

She sounded so remorseful Maggie laughed. "No hard feelings. If I were in your place I'd do the same thing."

But Marta's comment bothered her. *I don't think there's anything casual there.* She couldn't shake the feeling she was headed for emotional disaster—again.

Maggie knew she'd dodged a bullet, so to speak, since Ellen made no leading comments or dropped hints during Thanksgiving dinner. She hoped the older woman had finally realized Maggie was the wrong woman for Josh.

It hurt a little, but it was for the best.

Now, the next morning, she sat with her laptop, indulging in a little retail therapy. Cody and her friend Kerry's kids would benefit on Christmas.

"You coming on the Christmas-tree trip?" Josh asked from her doorway, coffee mug in hand.

Maggie looked up. He looked way too good in a Henley shirt that hugged his chest and shoulders. She swallowed hard.

"I'm not sure," she said. "Isn't it a family outing?"

He shrugged. "I don't mind. I can always use another set of eyes to make sure I don't get a crooked tree. Plus

Cody would love it if you came along." He sipped his coffee and raised an eyebrow.

She'd love a little tree for this room. She offered what she hoped passed for a neutral smile as she caved. "Thank you. I'd love to go."

"All right then. Sounds good." Josh pushed off the door frame. "We'll head out about eleven."

She glanced at the clock. It gave her an hour. She put the computer aside and surveyed her space. Where to put the tree?

Her phone rang as she dragged her sofa over. A glance at the display revealed Kerry's name.

"Hey," she greeted her friend. "Happy belated Thanksgiving."

Kerry laughed, and Maggie felt the tug of homesickness. "Same to you. So how was it with the hot doc?"

Maggie's face burned and she glanced at the door. Clearly, Josh couldn't hear. Still. She got up to close it. "Um. It was good. Ellen is a fantastic cook. Kerry—"

"I know, I know. Sorry." A sigh. "It's just I'm so hopeful for you."

Trust her friend to cut to the chase. "Ah. Well." Maggie went into her bathroom and got a garbage bag to put the tree stand on. Shoot. Tree stand. She didn't have one. Maybe there was an extra here. "Don't be."

Kerry made a sharp noise in her throat. "I thought we talked about this. Don't let Tony win."

"This isn't about Tony." It was true. Any hold he'd had over her was gone. As soon as Josh had looked at her like she was something special any residual hold Tony held over her shattered. Maybe it was silly, but she owed Josh for that boost of confidence.

"It's about Lucy."

Maggie nodded even though Kerry couldn't see her. "Bingo."

There was a moment of silence. "So there is something with you two."

No, there wasn't. The chances of that had been shot as soon as her father had chosen to keep his daughter secret and Maggie had picked those threads up.

"Listen, Kerry, I can't really talk right now. We're going to get Christmas trees."

"Hmm," Kerry teased. "Is that a nanny-and-boss thing or a Maggie-and-Josh thing?"

"I don't know," Maggie whispered. The lines were so blurry, more so by the day. She didn't know which side of it she was on anymore. Or worse, which side she *wanted* to be on.

"Oh, honey. Call me when you can talk. Or do you want me to come visit?"

Maggie promised to call as soon as she could, and they disconnected. Distracted, she stood in the middle of her room and stared at the empty space where her tree would go.

Then she gave herself a little shake. Today she'd live in the moment. She'd enjoy the trip and the experience. It was likely this would be her only Christmas here. She'd make the most of every moment.

Cody was ready. Boots, hat, warm mittens and coat were the order of the day, as a bitter wind blew outside even though it was sunny out. "You look warm," Maggie said, and Cody nodded.

"We're gonna get a big tree," he said, stretching his arms out wide. "Super-duper big."

Maggie widened her eyes. "Wow, that big, huh?"

Cody nodded, all serious. "Yep. An' then we can put all the stuff on it."

Maggie hid a smile. "Ornaments, you mean?"

Another nod. "And lotsa lights. Daddy said we gotta do those first."

"It makes it easier," Maggie agreed. "It sounds like you guys are going to have a lot of fun with your tree."

Cody frowned. "Aren't you gonna help?"

Maggie couldn't breathe for a second.

"I— Well, I'll have my own tree to decorate," she explained. "And you and your dad, well, you might want to do it by yourselves."

The frown deepened. "So I can't help you?"

Maggie crouched down in front of the little boy and looked into his worried eyes. She sure was making a mess of this, wasn't she? "Of course you can, if it's okay with your daddy. I'd love to have you help."

"'Kay. So you help us an' we'll help you," Cody said as if it were settled. Before she could say anything, Josh spoke from behind her.

"If you guys are ready, let's head out."

The radio tuned to a Christmas music station, they drove to a local Christmas tree farm. Cody sang along, a few words behind, and only a few he actually knew. It made Maggie's soul warm.

The drive was all too short, as far as she was concerned. Driving through the farm's gate, they parked in the already packed lot.

"Wow," Maggie said, observing the controlled chaos. "They don't mess around." Rows of cut trees, racks of fresh wreaths and garland, red ribbons and twinkling lights gave it a festive air.

Josh shook his head. "They don't. They work on this

like crazy. Have for a couple generations. This is owned by Jake's family." He sent her a sideways glance.

It took her a second, then she stifled a smile. "Is it, now? Well, maybe he's here." She hopped out of the SUV and allowed the grin to blossom for an instant. Was he…jealous?

She shook herself. It didn't matter.

Josh came around the hood. "You want to walk through the trees in the field? Or get one here?"

Their feet crunched on the gravel of the parking lot as they started walking. The wind whipped around them. "If they're fresh, I'm happy with one of those," Maggie said, eyeing the already cut trees lining the pole barn.

Cody stopped in front of her. He patted the first tree they came to, a short spruce, and looked expectantly at his dad. "This one?"

Josh shook his head. "We need a bigger one, Code. Bigger than me."

Cody looked up at his dad, eyes wide. "That's huge, Daddy." Maggie laughed outright and Josh tapped his son lightly on the head.

"And don't you forget it, mister," he teased. "Let's go look in here."

She followed them into the big barn. It couldn't claim to be warmer but at least it blocked the wind. She perused the smaller trees, enjoying the task. Cody darted between her and Josh, giving his opinions—the tree she liked wasn't big enough, but it was okay with him anyway because she liked it—and basically hyped up on the excitement that the errand and the season brought out in kids.

"Maggie." Josh stuck his head out from behind a tall tree. "Got a second?" Without waiting for an answer, he tugged her deeper into the miniforest. "I need help. This fir—" he indicated a tall graceful tree "—or this spruce?"

"Ahhh." Maggie reached out and touched both trees,

feeling the softness of the fir, the prickliness of the spruce and inhaled the sharp, heady scent of pine and Josh. What she wouldn't give to slip into his arms right now. She took a small step away to focus. "I'm partial to blue spruce, myself," she said. "It's what I picked out. I know firs hold their needles better but I love the blue color."

"Okay. Blue spruce it is," he said.

Startled, her gaze flew to his. "Oh. Josh, it's your tree—"

"Yours, too," he interrupted. "Cody doesn't care. And I want you to enjoy it, too."

Before Maggie could reply, Jake came up to them.

"Hey, Maggie. Josh." He nodded at both of them. There was no awkwardness in Jake's demeanor but Maggie felt Josh tense slightly.

"Jake." She smiled at him. "I didn't know you owned a farm until today."

"My parents do," he replied. "I work here every year, during the season. It's fun. And they love it. So what's your choice?"

"This one." Josh touched the spruce. "Maggie's got one, too."

"Okay. Let's get them together." He lifted the big tree and carried it out of the barn, Cody following watchfully. He set it by the baler and turned to Maggie. "Where's yours?"

"Right over here." She led the way to the small tree. Would he say anything?

"So that's how it is," he murmured behind her.

She shook her head, but he touched her arm. "Maggie. It's all over your face. His, too." He hefted the tree and gave her a quick grin. "I never stood a chance."

Dismayed, she looked up at him. "Oh, Jake—"

"No, it's okay, Maggie. No hard feelings. You were clear

on what you wanted. I pushed anyway. Now let's get you guys squared away."

Maggie followed him through the maze of trees. When they emerged, Josh's eyes went straight to her, and Jake said softly, "See?"

No. She didn't. She couldn't. To see it would mean she was in worse trouble than she thought.

And where would she be then?

Josh didn't ask what Jake said to Maggie in the trees, but he chewed on it most of the way home.

He couldn't be jealous.

Now, grinding his teeth, he tried not to stare at the curve of Maggie's ass as she went up the stairs while he hauled her tree along behind her.

It was a losing battle, like so much else when it came to her these days.

He carried Maggie's tree into her room. She'd already spread a garbage bag on the carpet in front of the French doors and had the stand they'd found in the garage ready. He wrestled the tree into the metal stand and came over to stand beside her. The sharp scent of pine mingled with the fruity scent of her hair. Distracted, his arm brushed hers and the shot of heat sidetracked him for a moment.

"It's got a curve," she said and the pout in her voice made him grin.

"You didn't see it at the farm?"

"No." She shot him a look. "Did you?"

He chuckled. "No. I didn't. We can probably adjust it some to make it straighter."

She crossed her arms. "It's silly. No one's going to see it but me. It doesn't matter if it's off-kilter."

"We can adjust it," he repeated. "No big deal. Give me a hand here? It's easier with two people."

She pulled on the old leather gloves he'd given her then stuck her hand into the tree. She held the trunk while he crawled on the floor underneath. They tweaked and adjusted and after a few minutes, Maggie stepped back and said, "There!"

He peered at her from under the tree, where he had a great view of her breasts. He'd never known a turtleneck sweater could be so sexy. *Focus.* "It's okay?"

"Perfect." Then she laughed, which made those breasts bounce. His focus skewed again. "If you tilt your head just a little, that is."

He screwed in the last of the pins and slid out to stand beside her. He gave it a semicritical eye and nodded. "I agree. Perfect." He dropped a kiss on her head without thinking. She went still and looked up at him, her eyes wide. His gaze latched on hers and he could barely breathe. The moment hung there, suspended, a crossroads.

What the hell. Cody was downstairs with his grandmother, which was reason enough to pull away. But God help him, he didn't want to.

Trav's words came back to him. *Why are you hiding?* Heart pounding, he turned to face her. She didn't move, but he saw the rapid rise and fall of her breasts under her snug little sweater. He slid his shaking fingers under her chin and lifted it. Her lips parted slightly and her gaze stayed locked on his. In those blue, blue eyes he saw heat and fear. He just wanted a taste of her to slake the thirst and need that burned him from the inside. Keeping his eyes open, he pulled her in closer and settled his mouth on hers lightly. Her hands landed on his chest, fisting in his shirt, but she didn't pull away.

He fully intended to stop there. Then she made a sound, low in her throat as her eyes drifted shut and she pressed against him. His control, already thin when it came to her, evaporated. *To hell with a taste.* He wanted the whole damn feast. He deepened the kiss, sliding his tongue in to meet hers, even as a part of his brain screamed for him to pull away.

He couldn't even if he'd wanted to. She was sweet and hot and every bit as hungry as he was. He shucked the leather gloves he still wore and wound one hand in her hair, the silky strands sliding over his skin. Her arms came around his neck, and the kiss got deeper, hotter, more urgent.

Cody's laughter came up the stairs, and she wrenched back. They stared at each other, breathing hard, and his heart sank as horror slid across her face. *Moment shattered.*

"Maggie—" Would it be better if he apologized or not? "I'm sorry." Not for the kiss, but for how he'd crossed her line. Hell, his own line.

She shook her head and stepped back. He let her go, though all he wanted was to pull her closer and kiss away the fear. She whispered, "I think it's best you go, Josh."

He knew she was right. Heart pounding, hormones roaring, he grabbed his gloves from the floor and walked out. The hell of it was, *a little taste* would never be enough. He hadn't banked the fire, he'd stoked it. And worse, hadn't he just busted his promise wide-open?

Chapter Nine

Maggie held it together until he left. She pressed both hands to her face and sank to the floor. What had she been thinking? As soon as she'd seen the intent on Josh's face, she should have stepped away. *But oh, the man could kiss.* She could still taste him on her lips. A traitorous little zing ran through her body.

She'd been caught by the moment, by her own wanting. Oh, she was weak and foolish. And—*Lucy.*

Despite the fire in her body, the fire only Josh could both build and extinguish, her guilt crested. They were on some kind of a crash course and Maggie didn't know how to stop it.

She had to tell him. Everything was spiraling out of her control and she didn't know how to stop it.

Cody's laughter and Ellen's quiet voice reached her ears and she shut her eyes. She was so far in this now, to leave would create a hole in Cody's life. Somehow the whole thing had gotten away from her. She didn't have control of her feelings for Josh, wasn't sure when she'd lost it. Wasn't sure she'd ever had it.

She needed to tell him. How?

She stared unseeing now at the tree that had brought her such joy only a few minutes ago. This was not going as she'd planned. Oh, she had her relationship with Cody, the link to the sister she desperately wished she'd known, but…Josh. That kiss. She shut her eyes and took a deep breath, willing the hormones to settle. It wasn't that easy, though. What she felt was far more than simple hormones. No, this was far more powerful, more dangerous.

Thumping on the stairs brought her to her feet moments before Cody burst in.

"Maggie! We're ready! Are you?"

She gave a little laugh, grateful Cody's excitement kept him from noticing her distress. "Ready for what?"

He did a little dance in place. "The Christmas tree is goin' up! Daddy's gonna bring it in. Gramma told me to get you. You comin'?"

Her heart sank even as she smiled at Cody. Ellen and her far too perceptive eyes would be a problem. She'd need to compose herself. "Of course I am. Be down in a minute or so, okay?"

"Okay!" Cody headed out at a dead run, shouting the good news to the adults downstairs.

She slipped into the bathroom, examined her flushed face in the mirror. She touched her mouth lightly and a little shiver slid through her. She could still taste him and feel the delicious hot pressure of his mouth claiming hers.

She wanted more. So much more.

Guilt speared her as she turned on the cold water and splashed it on her face, hoping to tame the redness. She toweled off and met her own somber gaze in the mirror again. This was getting rapidly out of hand yet they seemed unable to put the brakes on. Maybe she needed to move out? Get some distance from him, to help things cool off?

No. What she needed to do was tell him. Soon.

Then there'd be nothing left between them.

But she'd lose Cody, as well. That fact tore her up inside.

He was cutting it close.

* * *

Josh parked in his driveway Saturday evening and climbed out, hoping Maggie and Cody were nearly ready. He'd been longer than he anticipated when he'd been called in to the hospital, but he'd made it home under the wire.

"So. Who's up for the parade tonight?" he called when he opened the kitchen door.

"Me!" Cody cried, running around the corner. "I wanna go!"

Josh turned to Maggie. "There's one. Maggie?"

She hesitated and he was pretty sure he knew the reason. The awkwardness of their kiss yesterday hadn't faded. Still, every time he looked at her, he had to stop himself from reaching for her, kissing her again. Even though he knew how wrong it all was.

It was a special kind of hell.

"You should see the parade," he told her quietly. "It's a big deal."

Her gaze bounced off his, settled on Cody. "Okay."

Relief and frustration flowed through him. He didn't know how to fix this, how to make things comfortable again. He knew he'd messed up on several levels by kissing her, but God help him he'd do it again if he had the chance.

What was wrong with him?

He tried to put it out of his mind as they all got into coats and boots and started out to walk the two blocks to the main street and parade route.

It couldn't be a more perfect evening. A light snow had been sifting down most of the day, laying down a couple inches and still falling gently. Cody spun with delight through the gathering darkness and tried to catch flakes on his tongue. Maggie laughed at him and the low sound was both balm and aphrodisiac.

Maggie. He tried not to be so aware of her. Her dark

hair was loose under her bright pink hat and spilled on her shoulders. Their arms brushed on occasion, thanks to their coats and the narrow sidewalks, and once their hands touched. Hers were encased in thick mittens, and his in gloves, so he couldn't catch her fingers in his own as he feared he might have otherwise.

Just as well. But still, his hand itched to take hers. It seemed so right.

In a way he'd never felt with Lucy. Always, the chaos of their relationship had wiped out any chance for peace between them. A sliver of guilt slipped in, and with effort he pushed it aside. He didn't want to feel guilt. But it'd been with him so long he didn't know what else to feel.

They joined the crowd at the end of the street. He lifted Cody on his shoulders so the little boy could see better, and Maggie stood in front of them, her back to his chest.

The press of people around them had them standing tightly and Josh's attention wasn't on the parade, but on her. The silky strands of her hair brushed his jacket every time she moved her head. It was a damn good thing Cody was on his shoulders so his hands were occupied.

The floats drifted past, cheery with bright lights, bows and Christmas music. Santa hats and jingling bells were the order of the evening. Maggie replaced hers with a Santa hat handed to her by a merry old elf and turned to show Cody, laughter on her face and in her eyes. She was so beautiful Josh's breath caught. Something in him loosened a touch, warmed, and he felt the promise he'd made Lucy weaken even more.

God help him, right now he just wanted to kiss her.

The sounds, the lights faded away as they stood there, caught in their own world. It couldn't have been more than a heartbeat or two before she blinked, blushed and turned back to the parade.

Cody wiggled, and he put his son down.

"Can I sit there?" he asked, pointing at an opening on the curb in front of them.

"Sure," Josh said. "Stay seated, though."

"Okay." Cody settled between two other kids.

His hands were no longer occupied.

The hell with it.

He took advantage of the fact that it was dark and slid one hand on Maggie's hip to pull her against him. When she stiffened, he murmured in her ear, "Relax. No one can see."

She leaned on him slightly, close enough he could almost rest his chin on the top of her head.

He could have been in high school again, on a first date. The same giddy expectations coursed through him, this time, though, chased by a very adult lust. By a wanting so strong he knew it'd undo him.

She shifted again, just a hair, but enough that their bodies didn't touch anymore. He let her go, sensing that if he pushed it—especially in public like this—she'd withdraw even more. Still, he missed the contact, no matter how slight it had been.

Cody darted back from the curb. His eyes were huge and despite the dim light, Josh could see the sparkle in them. Maggie bent down to talk to Cody just as someone jostled Josh from behind. To keep from bumping her, he placed a hand lightly on her back.

These casual touches were going to drive him crazy. Especially since a lot of what he felt now he'd never felt in his marriage to Lucy. It was so…disloyal, to look at Maggie and feel what he did.

"Daddy! It's done! Can we go watch them light the tree?" Cody tugged on his hand, jumping up and down, excitement shining on his face. He pulled himself out of the past with effort and smiled at his son.

"Yep, we'd better hurry," he said. "As soon as it lights, we've got to head home and get ready for our part, okay?"

"Okay!" Cody boomed and grabbed his hand and Maggie's, too.

Linked by Cody, they walked toward the town square. They hefted Cody between them, letting him swing from their hands while the little boy laughed. Something swelled in Josh as they walked along. They were, for now, a family. To anyone who didn't know, they were a mom and dad and son on a special night.

Except they weren't.

Marta materialized in his line of vision. She smiled when she saw him, then looked surprised and delighted as she took in Maggie and Cody. He could see the wheels turning in her head. Hadn't he just been thinking they looked like a family? What would everyone else think?

As if sensing his thoughts, Maggie withdrew her hand from Cody's and slipped hers in her pockets.

"Hi, guys," Marta said, her knowing gaze sliding from Josh to Maggie. "Good to see you here." She linked her arm through Maggie's. "What did you think so far?"

Josh didn't hear Maggie's reply as the announcements began that it was time to light the tree. On the count of three, as the high school band broke in to "Joy to the World," the tall spruce lit up with gold and red lights. The onlookers cheered and clapped, Maggie among them.

"All right," he said over the noise to Maggie and Cody. "Let's go. We've got twenty minutes to get back and get everything ready to light up."

"Can't wait! We'll see you guys there," Marta said.

"Yeah!" Cody said, jumping up and down. "Do I get to plug in stuff, too?"

"Ahh," Maggie said, with a glance at Josh as they hurried back toward home. He shook his head. "I'm thinking no. But there are other things you can do."

"Like what?" Cody asked, clearly interested in spite of his disappointment. She smiled at him, wishing, like she had all evening, that things were simpler and they could just be a family enjoying the evening.

"Make sure things light up," Maggie said. "Or hand your dad the cords, maybe. It'll be quick and fun. But I'd think you'd want to be where you can see what's happening. Almost all the houses will light up at once, right? I think the place to be is on the sidewalk."

Cody considered that, then nodded. "Okay. Gramma is coming, too?"

"Yeah," Josh said. "She should be there when we get back. She wouldn't miss this for anything."

Ten minutes later, they were on the steps of the house, Ellen opening the door. "Right on time," she called. "Come on in. I've got hot chocolate ready. I know how cold it is out there. You've got a minute to take a few sips before heading back out." She closed the door behind them and hustled everyone in the kitchen.

Josh dropped a kiss on his mother's head. "I'll get some after we're all lit up, Mom. Thanks. I've got to go check all my cords. Cody, you want to come?" He went out in the garage with his son, whistling a Christmas tune as he went. Ellen rolled her eyes at Maggie.

"Boys. And electricity. What is it?" she asked with a laugh as she poured some hot chocolate in a travel mug for Maggie. "Here. This will warm you up."

Maggie could think of a dozen other things that would warm her up, starting with Josh's touch on her hip again. She hoped her cheeks were already pink as she accepted the mug and took a sip.

"Mmm." She sighed as the warm liquid slid down her throat. "This isn't from a packet."

Ellen laughed. "Of course not. Now let's go watch this place light up. It's quite a sight."

Maggie set her mug down long enough to zip her coat back up. "I can't wait. It was a lot of fun to set up," she said.

Ellen nodded and hesitated. She gave Maggie a long look that had her stomach tightening. "My son lights up," she said finally, "when he's around you. I don't know if he knows it. But I do know it's something I haven't seen in him in years. Maybe ever."

Maggie nearly dropped her cup. "But—his wife—" *My sister,* she couldn't say. How could this be fair?

"I can't comment on their marriage," Ellen said softly. "That's for Josh to tell you. I didn't see much of it, really. But I do know what I see on his face when he looks at you when he thinks no one's looking." She reached over and patted Maggie's hand. "He's a good man, a very good one. I'd say that even if he weren't my own son."

A very good man. Maggie thought of his mouth on hers the other day, of how wonderfully he treated his son and mother. Sexy. Honorable. Strong. An incredible combination. She found her voice over the pain that bloomed in her heart. "He is a good man. Well, I'm, um, not looking for a…man right now. I recently came out of a bad marriage and nasty divorce and I'm not up for another try." Not that Ellen had mentioned marriage, of course. And why was she thinking about that anyway?

"I can understand that," Ellen said. "Now let's go out front for the party, shall we?"

Maggie watched her walk out and clutched her mug of cocoa as if it were the Holy Grail. Or maybe her sanity. If it weren't for Cody, her sense of responsibility and the fact she was related to the little boy, she'd give notice and go find a teaching job somewhere.

Unfortunately, she found herself in the same situation that had landed her in so much trouble the first time—getting involved with the boss. She thought again of the kiss they'd shared the day before and a little shiver ran up her spine. They'd crossed the line and she didn't know how to go back. Or if they even could.

"Maggie!" Cody's excited voice snapped Maggie out of her thoughts and back to the festivities at hand. "It's time, Daddy said! C'mon."

Laughing, Maggie let Cody pull her toward the sidewalk where dozens of other people waited, enjoying the feel of his little hand in hers—even through mittens—and his visible excitement.

Ellen glanced at her watch as Maggie and Cody joined her and Marta. "Less than one minute now," she said. Sure enough, a few seconds later, the whole street lit up as every house on both sides of the street plugged in their Christmas displays at once. Cody squealed with delight and Maggie's gasp was lost in the collective gasp of the crowd.

"Wow," was all she could say. Next to her, Marta grinned and elbowed Maggie.

"Told you," she said.

Josh crossed the lawn, grinning and glancing backward at the house. "Every year I expect a *Christmas Vacation*-like scene where they blow every fuse in the county," he said when he reached them. "It's never happened, though. People are pretty serious about this." He brushed a lock of her hair out of her face, his cold fingers still leaving a burning trail in their wake. "What do you think?" He stood, tall and solid and warm, a boyish grin—not unlike Cody's—lighting his handsome features. Maggie's mouth went dry.

She managed to recover enough to say, "I think this is

amazing. I have never seen anything like it. You do this every year?"

He nodded. "Every year, after the parade. It's gone on for years and now it's a huge event, as you can see." He inclined his head toward the sidewalk, where Cody, Ellen, Marta, Trav and JT had already moved on. "Do you want to walk? We usually take a little tour of all the displays."

"That would be great." She fell into step beside him in the dark, though it was pretty well lit by the glowing houses and reindeer and Frosties and blow-up snow globes. "Wow, some people really take this stuff seriously, huh?" she said, stopping in front of a particularly busy display.

Josh laughed. "Very. Me, not so much. It's fun, for me and for Cody and for the whole street, but I just don't have the time to put into it that some people do."

"Well, you did pretty well," Maggie said, thinking the big blue house with its roof outlines and porch wrapped in color was the prettiest one she'd seen.

Maybe she was a teeny bit biased.

Josh took her arm and tucked it in his, pulling her against his side. "You helped."

Heat burned through Maggie at the gesture. Even through their heavy coats, she felt the warmth of his body and oh, how she wanted more. Which meant she needed to pull away before he fuzzed her brain to the point she chucked all her reasons for *why not* and just jumped him.

She let her hand rest lightly on his arm, trying to keep a bit of distance between them and therefore her sanity. But as much as she knew she needed to move away she enjoyed the contact too much. It couldn't hurt anything.

Right?

They gathered in the kitchen for one more cup of some-thing warm after Cody had gone to bed. It had taken a while to settle him down enough to lie down, but eventually he'd crashed. Ellen yawned and rose to carry her mug to the sink.

"I'm going to head on home," she said. "It's getting late. I'll see you kids later, okay?"

After Ellen had left, Maggie rose and took her own mug to the sink. "I think I'll go to bed, too," she said and gasped when Josh plucked the mug from her fingers and turned her around so she was back against the counter. "Josh? What—?"

But before she could finish his mouth was on hers, hot and wet and soft and hard. She stood frozen for a heartbeat then found herself opening beneath him—her arms went around his neck and she pressed against him, feeling his hardness and the bulge in his pants that pressed against her belly. She whimpered as his tongue plundered her mouth, as his hands slid down her sides then back up to brush her breasts. She arched at the little licks of fire that nipped along her nerves, wanting him.

Oh, God, how she wanted him.

He left her mouth and nibbled and nipped and sucked his way down her neck. She tilted her head back, grasping his shoulders, to give him better access.

"Maggie," he whispered against her skin, his breath hot, the roughness in his voice making the heat in her center ratchet up. He slid his hands under her shirt as she reclaimed his mouth and tugged at his shirt as well, wanting to feel his skin, his smooth hot skin, under her hands and against her own. He pulled her shirt up over her head, tossed it who-knew-where and lifted her up so she sat on the granite counter. He stood between her legs and pulled her against him. When the catch on her bra stuck, she pushed his hands out of the way and released it herself, so her breasts sprang right into his hands, right where they ached to be.

"You are so beautiful," he rasped, hands and mouth and tongue on her breasts, kneading, sucking, nipping as she struggled to contain her cries. His shirt came off, and he pulled her against him, so for a long moment they were skin on skin, and she could feel the pounding of his heart matched her own. It felt so good—so good, so right to be cradled against the chest of this man.

He lifted his hands to cup her breasts, teasing her sensitive nipples with his thumbs, then his teeth. He quickly eased her out of her jeans and slid one hand to her thigh, then slipped up, higher, higher until he'd touched her center through her panties. She gasped with the shock of his cold finger and gripped his bare shoulders. With a groan, he pushed the scrap of fabric away and slid a finger inside her, stoking the fire, the pressure building, building as he rubbed and nibbled and stroked and finally clamped his mouth on hers as she shattered around his fingers, the scream of his name swallowed in the heat of his kiss. Maggie clutched him, barely swallowing her cries, her body wracked with tremors and the realization she wasn't done, she wanted him again, inside her, and hell if she wasn't ready to do it right there on the counter—

—when she heard Cody start to cry.

Reality and shame crashed into her. Oh, God, *Lucy*.

Josh groaned and blinked. "That's my cue. Oh, God, Maggie, I'm sorry. I didn't mean to let it get out of hand."

She waved a hand as she slid off the counter—how was she going to work in here tomorrow knowing what they'd done right here? What they'd very nearly done, might have if Cody hadn't woken up?

And he was sorry. Of course. So was she.

"Well, we'll just forget it happened," she said, forcing a

calm note in her voice that was at odds with her suddenly melancholy mood and her still-burning desire.

Pathetic. He'd just made it clear it had all been a mistake and she wanted nothing more than to take him up to her room and finish it.

To forget who she was and the fact that she couldn't have him. Ever.

Josh took a step toward her as she retrieved her jeans from the sink. "Maggie, I—" Cody's cries increased in intensity. He shoved his hand through his hair. "Hell. Hold on." He headed for the stairs and she couldn't help but notice that he moved a little more stiffly than usual.

She found her shirt in front of the refrigerator, yanked it over her head and ran for her room. As she slid past Cody's room, she heard the low rumble of Josh's voice, soothing the little boy, whose sobs Maggie could hear through the door. Her heart constricted in her chest and shame flooded her. She'd let her guard slip for just a moment—okay, for a lot of moments—and had been all over Josh like he'd been coated in Godiva chocolate.

Which was wrong on so many levels Maggie didn't know where to start. Maybe she could start at the part that said there was a four-year-old child in the house and end with the fact she was Josh's sister-in-law.

And that pretty much summed it up.

Josh didn't bother to knock on Maggie's closed door after he'd settled Cody back down, even though he badly wanted to finish what they'd started.

But did she?

He knew he'd botched it. Knew he should have kept his hands to himself but hell if he could. She'd been so close to him all night, his control had flat-out snapped. *Inexcusable.*

At this rate, he'd be lucky if she stayed on the job. He cursed silently. They didn't want anything to happen, couldn't have anything happen, yet they continually toed the razor's edge. How would he find a new nanny if she quit? What would he do if she quit?

Layered in that question was another. What would he do, personally, if she quit? He couldn't imagine not having her around. She belonged here. Fit like she was the missing piece—one he hadn't even realized *was* missing.

The realization made him feel a little sick. He was headed full throttle down an unknown road, this time with Cody in tow. The consequences of failure were much bigger.

Fear swamped him. Chances were he'd fail again. He'd proven with Lucy he wasn't a good husband. She'd died trying to get away from him and their marriage, for God's sake. It didn't get any worse than that.

Still, he feared he'd gone too far to turn back now.

Chapter Ten

If anyone guessed how Josh spent his Saturday night, no one commented. Though of all his employees only Marta would say anything, and only then because Josh and her husband were such good friends. Still, she kept quiet and Josh hoped he'd gotten off the hook.

Though clearly knowledge of Maggie and speculation about their relationship was getting around town. He'd been urged by three of his patients today to give their assorted female relatives a call soon because *she was such a lovely woman.* He'd been hit on by one other patient—not on the level of Julie Henney, thankfully, but still a waste of time on his end and hers.

The one woman he wanted—and there was no denying it now—was the one he couldn't have.

Marta breezed in. "Wow, you must really have made an impression with Maggie at the parade this weekend. We've got eligible women and their champions lined up all day. Tomorrow, too," she added, giving him a grin. "They're worried you're going to go to an outsider."

Josh leaned back in his chair, annoyance warring with humor inside him. "Like I'm the grand-prize pig at the county fair?" he said wryly, and Marta shrugged.

"You know how this works. They all want to be responsible for healing your broken heart."

Josh thumped the chair legs back down on the floor. "Marta—"

She held up a hand. "I know the score, doc. But other than me and Trav? I don't think anyone knows what things were like with you and Lucy. Does your mom even know?"

Did she? Josh never said in so many words, but he was pretty sure they'd been giving off bad vibes for the entire marriage. "I don't know. She's never asked. Or said anything."

Marta shrugged. "It wouldn't matter anyway. A commitment-shy widower is just as good as a heartbroken widower in the eyes of those who would save you. Maybe even more of a trophy," she added, then grinned when his eyes narrowed. "Maybe you could compete with that grand-prize pig, after all."

Josh choked on a laugh, because he knew enough about some female minds to know what Marta said held some truth. Senseless, but true. "Thanks, Marta. What would I do without you to keep my ego in check?"

She laughed, then sent him a pointed look on her way out the door. "Find your own woman to do it for you."

Ah, the sticking point. Even though he was wildly attracted to Maggie, he couldn't take what had happened any further.

But he wanted more. Much more. He wanted Maggie in his bed every night. He *wanted* the elusive commitment Marta was so sure he wanted to avoid. It wasn't going to be. The sooner he accepted he couldn't have Maggie, not now, not ever, the better off he'd be. Things could go back to how they were. Normal. Safe.

Somehow the whole idea rang hollow instead of being comforting.

When he got home that night, he found Maggie and Cody sitting down to decorate freshly baked Christmas cutout cookies. Cody sat at the table in front of a sheet of wax paper, a pile of unfrosted cookies nearby and surrounded by red and green sugars, plus little festive decorator things of all sizes and colors. Christmas music played from the small radio in the kitchen. It was a festive, warm, family scene. Maggie gave him a small nod as she stirred what looked to be icing in a small bowl. Her cheeks turned the faintest hint of pink and he longed to kiss her. With effort he tore his gaze away and switched it to Cody.

His son kneeled on the chair. "Look, Daddy! We baked 'em, now we get to frost 'em. Then I can eat one!"

"Really?" Josh asked, stopping by his son's chair.

"Yeah! Maggie said."

"Just one?" Josh eyed the pile of unfrosted cookies. He'd bet there were five dozen unfrosted yet. They'd been busy today. Maybe Maggie had been expending nervous energy.

The thought cheered him.

"C'n you help?" Cody asked, his blue eyes wide. "We gots lots."

Josh chuckled. "Yeah, you do. Tell you what. Let me change and I'll be down in a few, okay? Don't wait for me," he added as he headed for the stairs.

Maggie focused on the bowl of icing so she didn't watch him walk away. It took far more effort than it should have. She'd worked so hard all day to keep thoughts of him at bay.

It had been a waste of time.

"C'n we frost one for Daddy?" Cody asked as he dumped red and green sprinkles on the cookie, then mashed them in with his fingers.

"As soon as he comes down," she promised and raised a brow as Cody lifted his fingers toward his mouth. "If you're going to lick them, you'll have to wash them," she reminded him.

Cody looked longingly at his fingers, then wiped them

on the sticky towel next to him and emitted a put-upon sigh. Maggie bit her lip to hide a smile.

She heard Josh coming down the stairs and her stomach flopped when he reentered the kitchen, dressed in a plain T-shirt and flannel pj bottoms—green with reindeer. Goodness, she was in trouble if the man could make flannel sexy. Her hand trembled slightly as she spread the drippy icing on another Christmas-tree cookie and placed it in front of Cody. The little boy carefully placed the cookie he'd just finished off to the side with his other colorful creations. So far, he was foregoing convention in favor of craziness.

"Nice tree," Josh commented as he took his place from across Maggie at the table. Cody piled the red sugar on and started to add little silver balls.

He gave his dad a huge smile. "Yep. Maggie'll do one for you, Daddy. We can share this stuff." He indicated the decorations with a wave of his hand.

"Sounds good." Josh smoothed the wax paper in front of him and smiled at Maggie when she placed another cookie in front of him. "Thanks," he said softly.

She gave him a quick smile as Cody launched into an animated description of their day.

So far, she'd done all right where Josh was concerned. She'd managed to keep her distance and be polite, friendly. Acting like nothing had ever happened, like there was nothing between them.

But oh, how hard it was.

She slid a frosted reindeer on his wax paper mat and he winked at her. Flustered, Maggie felt her color rise. This was no good. She needed to get a grip here, and fast. There could be no repeats of the other night under any circumstances, especially not the false ones they were operating under now.

And whose fault is that?

But as she watched Josh and Cody interact, watched Josh tease Cody, then tease her—and damn her for responding, even though it didn't help her keep her vital emotional distance—she realized it was already too late. She'd gotten in way over her head. She'd never intended to have any feelings for Josh—or to not tell him who she was.

If he knew, he'd have every right to send her packing.

She kept up the charade of frosting, laughing, all the while her heart ached at how wonderful Josh and Cody were together and the knowledge that no matter what, she couldn't be a part of it. It wasn't her place. Couldn't be.

She'd made sure of that inadvertently when she'd chosen to keep her identity from Josh.

Ellen walked in that evening as they were finishing up dinner. Maggie saw her eyes widen as her gaze swept over the dozens of cookies on the counter. She couldn't help but smile. They'd gotten them all done. Eaten would be another story. She started to rise and Ellen waved her off. "Please don't get up."

"Come sit down, Mom," Josh said as he rose to pull out a chair. "We're almost done. What brings you out tonight?"

She sat down and smiled at him. "I'd like to take Cody for the night."

Cody whooped and nearly jumped out of his chair. Maggie gave him a look, even as her heart sank. "Careful, Cody. You need to finish first."

He shoved his fork at the broccoli on his plate. "Even this stuff?"

"Even that," she said, keeping her voice steady, hoping no one could see her distress.

"Mom, are you sure? This is awful short notice," Josh said. She couldn't look at him, afraid of what she'd see. Of what he'd see.

She nodded. "I figured you two had shopping you

needed to do. And I enjoy spending the time with my grandson."

Maggie pushed back from the table, needing to escape. "I'll just go get his backpack ready," she murmured.

Up in his room, she grabbed Cody's jammies and clothes and tried to calm her buzzing nerves. Maybe she'd go to Hannah's to remove herself from temptation. She heard Cody on the stairs and smiled at him when he burst in. "I've got your clothes," she said. "Why don't you pick a couple friends, too? I wasn't sure who you'd want to take."

Cody grabbed Bear Bear, of course, and a stuffed rabbit named Bun. She put both of them in his backpack and followed him back downstairs.

She set the backpack next to Ellen, noting Josh looked a little strained. It didn't make her feel any better. "Here's his things. He's got his friends in here, too."

Ellen smiled up at her. "Thank you, dear." To Cody she said, "Get your snow things. It's coming down nicely out there. Maybe we can go out for a little bit when we get back to my house, okay?"

"Okay!" Cody bounced out of the kitchen, and Maggie heard him talking to himself as he gathered the necessary items. When he came back out, Ellen picked up the pack and smiled at them.

"Have a nice evening, you two. I'll bring him home after lunch."

Josh held out his arms to Cody. "Sounds good. Cody, have fun with Grandma."

"I will." Cody hugged him, then ran over to hug Maggie, as well. She hugged him tight, panic in her throat. They'd be alone. She didn't think she could handle that.

She went in the kitchen when they left and loaded the dishwasher almost blindly. Josh sat at the table very still. She couldn't look at him, afraid of what she'd see, or what she wouldn't.

Maybe she could just lock herself in her room for the evening, since she wasn't needed. She couldn't risk Josh guessing her feelings for him. The temptation of being alone was too great and her feelings too raw to risk letting her guard down.

But the elephant in the room was the attraction they clearly shared and hadn't hid so well. It needed to be addressed before either of them could go on.

Remembering what had transpired on this very counter, she blushed, then took a deep breath and decided to give both of them an easy out.

"Well, when I'm done here, I think I'll go see if Hannah needs any help," she said as cheerfully as possible. "That way there won't be any awkward moments. You—" She trailed off as Josh pushed his chair back and came over to her, his gaze never leaving her. Trapped, she couldn't look away. She was sure the mix of need and apprehension and fear she saw in his whiskey gaze was reflected from her own. The determination was his own.

He stopped short of touching her, but she felt the heat of his body all the same. "Stay. Please." The words were low and vibrated like a string stretched taut between them. She held one end—she could drop it and could walk away. He'd let her go.

Except, she couldn't. She wanted this so badly, what they both knew was so wrong for both of them, yet it seemed the harder they tried to resist, the more they were pulled together.

She swallowed. Lifted her chin and met his gaze firmly even as every nerve in her body trembled. "Okay."

He stepped back and she felt the loss of his nearness with both relief and frustration. "Want to take a walk?"

She blinked at him. Whatever she'd thought he'd say, that wasn't on the list. She looked out the window where snow was falling, albeit gently. Might be just the ticket to cool this thing between them. "Now?"

"Why not?" He nodded at the dishes. "This can wait."

She hesitated. What could possibly happen on a walk in the snow? It would be good to clear her head. Maybe get a grip on her emotions.

"Okay," she agreed.

He gave her a little smile. "Thank you."

She wiped her hands on a dish towel and took a deep breath to try and calm her jumping belly. *Just a walk.* There was nothing more to read into it. Slightly settled, she grabbed her coat.

They donned winter gear and boots in silence. Josh held the door for her and she walked out into the hush of the falling snow.

The undulating white blanket, already a good four inches of the fresh stuff, covered everything. She took a step. Josh grabbed her arm and Maggie stopped to look at him, surprised.

"Listen," he murmured in her ear. The hot brush of his breath sent a small shiver down her spine. "You can hear the snow falling."

Maggie tilted her head as he stepped away and listened. Sure enough, she could hear the steady, yet nearly silent, thrum of the falling flakes piling up.

They walked down the driveway. Maggie looked back at the house with the twinkle lights muted by the snow, giving off a Christmas-card glow.

It looked like home. But it wasn't hers, not really, no matter much how she wished it could be.

She lost her footing briefly and Josh offered her his arm with a raised eyebrow. She slipped her arm lightly through his and resolved not to think for the rest of the walk. Just feel and enjoy the precious gift of time with Josh.

"Pretty, isn't it?" Josh asked as they passed the other

houses, all lit up, and the snow crunched beneath their boots.

"Oh, yes. Magical," she decided. "It's like being in a snow globe."

He chuckled. "Agreed." They lapsed into a comfortable silence as they turned off on to Main Street and Maggie stopped with a little exclamation.

"It looks like a Christmas card." She laughed and gestured at the buildings with their caps of snow, all decorated with twinkle lights and pine boughs. "Any minute you expect to see a horse-drawn sleigh come right down the street."

"A sleigh, huh?" Josh looked thoughtful.

"Yeah. I've always wanted a ride in a sleigh. It seems so…cozy on a snowy day." She'd almost said *romantic*. Given what they were skating around, it seemed prudent to avoid the word.

They walked a little farther, past the closed but merrily dressed shops, to the park. The water was dark, with occasional snowy patches where ice had formed.

Josh tipped his head toward the water. "In a couple weeks, if it stays cold enough for the ice to form, the lake will be covered in ice shanties. Lots of fishermen."

"More business for you?" Maggie asked, and he laughed.

"Not really. The occasional fish-hook removal but for the most part as long as they don't fall through the ice, they're fine."

"That's good, then." Maggie tilted her face up to the gray sky, eyes closed, as the cold flakes hit her skin. When she opened them again, Josh's gaze was intent on her face.

Heat curled between them, lazy, but hot enough Maggie was sure the falling snow turned to steam. Her fingers curled into his sleeve as wanting slid through her, leaving a burning trail of need in its place. Warning bells were quickly snuffed out as Josh leaned down and settled his mouth on hers. All thought fled as her eyes drifted shut and she leaned into him.

His lips were cold but his mouth was hot. Clutching his jacket, she opened to him—who let out that moan?—and let her tongue mate with his as the barely banked fire roared through her body. He pressed harder and she pressed back, inviting him deeper, closer…wanting, needing to get as close as possible, but gloves and warm coats—no longer seeming necessary—prevented the skin-to-skin contact she craved like breath itself.

The rumble and roar of an approaching snowplow snapped Maggie to her senses, and she pulled away as the plow whooshed by, sending a pile of snow their way.

"I'm sorry," Josh said, his voice hoarse.

Maggie stepped away as pain curled though her. Every time he kissed her he apologized. She turned around to head back home. "Don't be. It was just the moment."

But, oh, what a lie. She wanted so much more than the moment, so much more that wasn't hers to take.

"Maggie—"

Maggie placed her finger over his lips and shook her head. "Please don't apologize," she said. To hear it again would break her heart. "It happened. We're both adults who are very attracted to each other. We'll control it. Let's just leave it at that, okay?"

She turned to walk away, but he caught her arm. *Darn him.* Ruining her dramatic exit. Such as it was.

"Damn it, Maggie." He stepped closer. "I'm not sorry about kissing you." He tipped her chin and her pulse picked up. "I'm sorry that damn plow came along and broke us up. That's all I'm sorry for." He rested his hands on her waist and tugged her closer. Maggie couldn't tear her gaze off his.

"Me, too," she whispered.

"I'm going to kiss you again," he murmured and the intent in his voice sent little sparky shocks to her core. "But I want to do it inside." Their gazes locked, and desire tangled between them. She could barely breathe. "Maggie, can I come upstairs with you?"

Maggie touched his cheek. She knew what he was asking, knew she wasn't strong enough to say no, knew she wanted this badly enough to risk it all. "Yes," she said, her voice strong, all uncertainty gone. His eyes flared and Maggie knew she'd answered his unspoken question. He took her hand and they left the park at a decidedly quicker pace than they'd entered it.

Tonight was all about the magic. Tomorrow—well, tomorrow she'd deal.

They'd barely gotten into the house when they came together, shrugging out of wet jackets and boots with low laughter and lingering kisses.

Maggie led him upstairs, hoping to regain her balance, to keep her heart out of this as much as possible. Even though it was far, far too late for that.

She flipped on the fireplace, and plugged in the Christmas tree. Then, nerves fluttering, she looked over at where he waited in the doorway.

"Are you sure?" His voice was low and rough but she knew he'd walk away if she told him no. It was that knowledge that allowed her to say yes.

"I'm sure. For tonight."

"For tonight," he murmured, and her already racing pulse skipped as he approached her with a predatory look in his eyes. He stopped in front of her, close enough she could feel his heat, and she nearly imploded with the need to touch him.

Who moved first, she couldn't say. Didn't care. Didn't matter, really. All that mattered was he kissed her as though if he didn't, he'd die. She opened up under him, welcoming his tongue, feeling it sweep her mouth, tangling with her own. Her hands fumbled with his shirt, finally yanking it free of his jeans, as he did the same to her, never breaking the kiss.

Skin, smooth over hard muscle, under her palms. Goose bumps rose on his skin under her touch and an answering tremor ran through her. *It's right, it's so right.* Then her ability to think flew out the window as he pulled her shirt over her head and opened her bra. She cried out as he took one nipple in his teeth, the other between his fingers, and worked them until she could barely stand. The heat and pressure low in her belly had her gasping.

"Josh! Oh, my God, please?" Her words came out on a whimper. God, she couldn't even think what she wanted to say but it probably was something along the lines of *take your pants off right now.* Or maybe just *take me right now.* She reached for his zipper but he caught her hand.

"I'll be right back. Before we go too far." He left the room. She heard some slamming then he was back.

"That was quick," she said with a grin as he stepped back into her arms.

"I don't want to waste a minute," he said and tossed the foil packages on the bed. "Where were we? Oh, yeah." He returned his attention to her breasts and she clutched at him as the peak came at her again. With a whimper, she clutched his shoulders.

"Wait," he whispered against her mouth and nipped her lower lip. "Not yet. Just a little longer." He eased her back onto the bed and she was more than happy to assist him in removing her jeans. Her undies—pink cotton, not really sexy—stayed on, though, so she lay spread before him clad only in those and suddenly felt shy. When she tried to cover herself up, though, he stopped her.

"Don't, Maggie. You're gorgeous." By the look in his eyes she could see he meant it. His gaze roamed over her, leaving her skin as hot as if he'd touched her. Then he did, easing her panties aside to slip his fingers in, hitting the sweet spot right on and the pressure…oh, the pressure that built and built and burst on her scream. As tremors wracked her body, she realized she wasn't even close to done. As she reached for him, his zipper, pulling his jeans and boxers down—oh, my God, holiday print boxers, who knew?—his erection sprang right into her hand and she slid her hand down the hot silkiness of it, hearing him grind out her name.

"Maggie," he gasped, a guttural sound, and gripped her shoulders. "Oh, honey, if you're going to— I'm going to—"

The heady sense of control took over. She pushed him so he went on his back. She tore open the package and slipped the condom down his length.

"Maggie," he managed to say as she swung her leg over him, hovering right above him, teasing them both with what they both wanted, leaning forward so her breasts were in reach of his mouth. He obliged her with a growl, first one then the other until, unable to stand it another second, she finally slid down his erection, taking him in, feeling him fill her, letting her heat surround his hardness. He felt so good, so *right*. She began to move, up and down as he rocked to match her for each thrust, his hands on her breasts, her mouth on his as they shattered together, while the snow fell, the fire crackled and the tree sparkled.

Chapter Eleven

They made love several times that night, waking and reaching out, finding in each other what had long been missing in both their lives. What Maggie never had, and feared she would never have again.

When she woke and found him gone an emptiness filled her soul, where for a just a few hours, Josh had been. The rumpled sheets and blankets told the story. Clothes tossed all over the floor, though his were gone—a testament to their eagerness last night. It both heated and shamed her to see the evidence of their lovemaking, to feel the evidence of it on and in her body. She'd never been so well and thoroughly loved. Ever.

Now it was over.

Which was as it should be. Her heart pinged. They'd crossed so many lines, broken so many rules, Maggie didn't even know where to start.

But they'd agreed, it would only be one night.

Which also was as it should be. He didn't belong to her, no matter how much she loved him.

With a sigh, she rose and padded to the bathroom. She needed a shower. Then she'd figure out how to face Josh and deal with the weirdness because it wasn't like they could avoid each other.

Kinda hard when his bedroom was a few steps from

hers. That thought opened the door for others she couldn't deal with, so she ruthlessly shut them down.

She cranked the hot water on and slipped in, let the water sluice over her, and enjoyed how deliciously sore she was in a very key place. No matter where they went from here, it had been the best night of her life. She'd treasure the memory always.

He's not yours.

As the guilt over her half sister flowed back in, she welcomed it. She needed the sting of the pain to keep her priorities straight. Namely, Cody. Not his father.

Somehow, they'd all gotten twisted together and she didn't know if she could separate one from the other without it all coming apart.

And right there was the problem with forgoing thinking in favor of feeling. Things got…emotionally messy.

Maggie toweled off after her shower. Still. She'd been unable to resist him and the opportunity to have one night. She simply wasn't strong enough.

Especially given what loomed on the horizon.

Ellen had promised to bring Cody back after lunch, so Maggie had a couple of hours to herself. Since the last thing she wanted was to be alone with her thoughts, she found herself walking down to Hannah's to see if there was anything she could do.

She knocked on the door and tucked her face into her collar to avoid the wind. Her body still hummed from the previous evening with Josh. If she shut her eyes she could feel his hands on her skin, his mouth…

Hannah pulled open the door, took one look at Maggie and frowned. "Everything okay?"

Maggie forced a smile. "Why wouldn't it be?"

Hannah stepped aside and let her in. "Not sure. You look…well, you look like you've got a lot on your mind."

Maggie's cheeks started to burn as she slipped out of her

coat. That was one way to put it. "I suppose I do," she said, unsure if she wanted to share what had happened or not.

I should have known better.

"Well, if you want to talk, I'm your girl." She opened a cupboard and took out two mugs. "Coffee? I was just taking a break."

"Sure," Maggie said, accepting the steaming cup.

Hannah sat down, then reached across the table to touch Maggie's hand. "What's going on? You look like you're going to fall apart."

Tears burned behind Maggie's eyes and she forced them back. "I've really screwed up."

Hannah sat back. "Oh? How's that?"

She shut her eyes. "I slept with Josh." The words were followed by both a thrill in her body and a wash of shame. She couldn't just box it up as one night. It made it less than it really was.

"Ah. I can't say I'm surprised, Maggie."

Maggie's gaze flew to Hannah's sympathetic one. This wasn't what she wanted to hear. "You're not?"

Hannah shook her head. "Nope. The two of you are positively sparky when you're together. I don't suppose you'd care to share details with someone who hasn't been there in ages?"

Maggie dropped her head into her hands. She couldn't share the magic, the wonder of it all, because she needed to keep it all locked up. "I can't."

"Damn. That's okay. But I have to ask, why is this a bad thing?"

Maggie stared into her coffee and was sorely tempted to unload the whole story. She could trust Hannah. But after so long holding on to it, where did she start? She took a deep breath.

"I was involved with my boss before. We got married, he cheated, I quit my teaching job after the divorce. I told you part of that before. Josh is my boss. I don't want to get in the same situation." She tightened her grip on the mug, glanced up. Hannah's expression grew sympathetic. "But. A lot…happened then. My father died and we found out he had another daughter. Before he'd met my mom. My mom and I didn't know."

Hannah sat back, stared. "Oh, Maggie." She reached over and grasped Maggie's fingers. Maggie closed her eyes as the tears pressed against her lids. She'd gone too far to back down now. "It was Lucy," she said on a sob, and felt Hannah's fingers go slack, then tighten.

"So you're—" Hannah said slowly, and Maggie nodded as the tears poured down her face.

"Lucy's half sister." Guilt, pain and remorse pulsed through her.

"Does Josh—?" Hannah asked and shook her head. "I can see by your face it's a no. Oh, Maggie, what were you thinking?"

There was no censure in her friend's voice, but the words hit her hard. "I wanted to get to know Cody. And not, you know, hurt them. I didn't know what it would do to them to show up out of the blue. I figured this was a safe way to do it. Especially since… Well, I know her mother never told her about my dad. Our dad." She shredded a paper napkin, her nervous fingers working it to tiny pieces. She didn't feel much better for the telling, knew she wouldn't until she told Josh.

She knew, too, when she did she'd lose them both. Could she risk it? To lose her whole family? Her father and sister to death, her mother to bitterness. Josh not wanting anything to do with Lucy's family. What a mess she'd created. The old saying was clearly true—the road to hell was certainly paved with good intentions.

"But," Hannah prompted, her voice still gentle.

Maggie shrugged as a fresh wave of tears broke over

her. Annoyed, she swiped them away. It was stupid to cry when she'd brought this on herself. "But there was Josh. And he was…well, he just was. Truthfully, I never considered him as part of the equation—Cody is my focus, Josh is my employer. Well, then we have this chemistry that's been building. Last night we took this amazing walk in the snow and it was like we were in this bubble of magic. And we…well, you know. Even though I knew it was wrong and it could not work. But I just don't know how to tell him."

Hannah sat back and studied Maggie for a long minute. "What are you most afraid of?"

Maggie thought of the tenderness in the way he'd loved her last night and squeezed her eyes shut against the memory. "Losing the connection with Cody. Losing Josh."

Hannah lifted her mug, set it down again. "You might lose them if you tell him. But if you don't tell him, and he finds out anyway, you'll lose them both for sure, Maggie. Is it worth the risk?"

Maggie locked her gaze on her friend's. There was the question she was wrestling with her conscience over. Really, the answer didn't matter—there was only one right answer and she knew what it was. "No. It's gotten away from me." Their relationship had grown so fast, blowing up like a midsummer thunderstorm.

Hannah sighed and nodded. "You've got a big mess here, honey. But I can see why you can't get involved with him—or think you can't. You've got to work through this. And you have to tell him. Sooner rather than later at this point."

Panic swamped Maggie. "What do I do, just walk up and say, 'Oh, by the way, I'm your sister-in-law?'"

Hannah shrugged. "However it comes out, is my guess. But what you're building here is based on a lie of omission, even though you didn't mean it to be. It'll be easier to rebuild if you tell him before it goes much further."

What Hannah said was absolutely true. Maggie knew that. She took a deep breath. "I will. But not until I can be sure I won't lose Cody. He's the reason I'm here. Hannah—" She paused, not sure how to ask her friend what she needed.

Hannah shook her head. "I won't say a word, Maggie. It's none of my business. But, sweetie? Don't wait too long." She reached over and squeezed Maggie's hand. "I'm here if you need me. Good luck."

Maggie knew all too well she'd need it.

When Ellen dropped off Cody, Maggie was reasonably composed. To Ellen's credit, she didn't ask any questions or even look too hard at Maggie.

Cody gave her a big hug when he came through the door. "Hi, Maggie."

"Hi, buddy." She squeezed him lightly. "You have fun?"

"Yeah. I got to stay up really late," he said proudly.

"Really?" Maggie looked at Ellen, who smiled back.

"Nine-thirty. Practically midnight."

Maggie laughed. "Especially when you're four. Thank you for bringing him home."

Ellen dropped one more kiss on Cody's head. "No problem. I enjoy having him. He's a joy."

Maggie agreed. No matter how this all worked out, she was so very grateful for the opportunity to get to know him—and Ellen, too.

Cody went into the living room to take stock of the loot under the tree. He checked periodically for new gifts, which always made Maggie smile.

Ellen left without any leading comments or too much small talk. Maggie heaved a silent sigh of relief. Did she dare hope Ellen hadn't picked up on the same vibes Hannah had?

God, she hoped not. Wouldn't that be awkward?

With a little shudder, she went and sat on the floor by Cody, who was examining a red-wrapped package with great intensity.

"I know you just got home, but we need to do a little Christmas shopping for your daddy and Gramma. Why don't you go to the bathroom and then we'll head out?"

"'Kay." He gave the package one last shake. "Legos," he announced. Maggie raised a brow and hid a smile.

"Really? How do you know?"

"It rattles," he said and replaced the present reluctantly, then got up.

As Cody scampered off, she watched him go with both love and trepidation in her heart. She loved the little boy with all her heart. How could she leave him?

The trip across town only took a few minutes. She and Cody had just entered the craft store when Maggie's cell phone rang. Digging through her purse, she pulled it out and frowned at the display. The number wasn't familiar.

"Hello?" she asked, guiding Cody toward hand print craft kits.

A pause. Then, "Is this Maggie Thelan?" The woman's voice was low, nervous.

"Yes. Who is this?" She didn't want to be rude but her creep meter was ringing.

"It's Jeanine. Jeanine Brooks."

Maggie nearly dropped the phone. Lucy's mother.

"I don't know if you remember me, but—" Her voice faded away.

"I do. I do. Of course I do. How are you?" Oh, dear. She sounded like a Dr. Seuss book.

The woman ignored her. "Do you think— I mean would you be able to meet me tonight? In Long Lake? I know it's short notice, but I'd like…well, to meet with you and that's about halfway." She finished in a rush, like she thought maybe she'd change her mind.

Maggie's brain whirled. She'd left Jeanine her cell number the first time she'd contacted her. The older woman had obviously hung on to it for a year. She'd also been very, very clear on not wanting to talk to Maggie. What had changed?

"If you don't want to, I understand," Jeanine said quietly. "I wasn't very nice to you the last time we talked."

"No, that's not it at all," Maggie said hastily. "I can. I'd love to. What time?"

They settled on seven, which meant she'd have to leave almost as soon as Josh got home. She clicked the phone shut, excitement and trepidation warring in her belly. What would she tell him?

"Who was that?"

She managed a smile for Cody. "Just someone I need to talk to later. So, which of these kits should we get? Do you want to make a stone for your Gramma's garden?"

Successfully distracted, Cody concentrated on the craft kits as she dropped her phone in her bag. She wished she could tell him who she was going to see. Cody didn't know his maternal grandparents and while she wished things were different, it wasn't her call.

Nerves skittered down her back. What did Jeanine want after rejecting Maggie so soundly a year ago?

She told Josh she had an appointment, which was true. Thankfully, he didn't ask her to elaborate. This also had the dubious benefit of getting her out of the house and away from him and all the leftover tensions from last night. They'd have to figure out how to deal with each other, but she couldn't do it now.

Maggie arrived at the little restaurant Jeanine mentioned fifteen minutes early. She seated herself in a booth next to the window, both so she could keep an eye on the parking lot and for its semiprivate nature.

Nerves twisted in her belly and she barely touched the coffee the waitress brought her. Jeanine had been crystal clear in her refusal to meet with Maggie the first time she'd contacted the older woman. Maggie had assumed she was simply unable to deal with her daughter's death and apologized for the intrusion into her life. She wasn't sure what to think about the out-of-the-blue contact now.

A silver coupe turned in and parked. Maggie kept her eyes on the car until its door opened and a trim woman stepped out.

She wore a slim gray suit with a bright floral scarf at her neck. Her hair was clipped short, a light brown with golden highlights. When she entered the restaurant she scanned it, then her gaze landed on Maggie.

No smile of welcome, just a determined look as she crossed the room. The butterflies increased tempo in Maggie's belly and she clasped her shaking hands in her lap for a moment.

"Hi, Jeanine," she said, pleased her voice stayed steady.

"Maggie. Thanks for meeting me here," she said.

"It's no problem," Maggie said as the waitress approached their table. She sat very still as the woman filled their cups. After she'd gone, Jeanine lifted her gaze to meet Maggie's. In the other woman's eyes Maggie saw pain and sorrow. She held her breath, afraid the wrong words would send Jeanine running.

"You look a little like her," Jeanine said softly, almost to herself. "The dark hair, the eyes." The pain sharpened in her eyes and caught at Maggie's heart. "From your father, of course."

Maggie didn't know how to respond. *Thank you* seemed inappropriate somehow.

"I guess you are wondering why I asked you to meet

me, after the last time," she said with a ghost of a smile. "You caught me completely off guard. I didn't know Frank had another daughter and truly I never thought of Lucy as having another family. I don't know why," she murmured, her gaze drifting off. "I just never did."

She took an absent sip of coffee. Maggie didn't speak, almost didn't dare to breathe.

"I don't know how much you know about Frank and me," she continued. "We met before he met your mom. I know that. I—" Here, her voice faltered, and she paused to swallow. "I was having a rough patch with my husband. We'd been married for a couple years, and were kind of going in different directions. We were awfully young," she murmured. "Right out of high school. We had no idea what being married was like." She laughed. "Like playing house, I thought. He'd go to work, come home to a hot meal I cooked, while the little ones sat with shiny clean faces around the table. Not quite."

As the story unfolded Maggie learned that, no, it hadn't gone that way at all. Hugh worked late hours and came home long after the hot meal had cooled. They rarely ate together, rarely even slept in the same bed. Jeanine felt invisible to her husband, and panicky because the much-anticipated babies were not arriving. So, she'd gone out one night when her husband wasn't home, and met Maggie's father at a bar. They left together and Jeanine, terrified and guilt-stricken, seduced her husband that same night because she somehow knew Frank had gotten her pregnant.

"He didn't know I was married," Jeanine said. She lifted her gaze to meet Maggie's. "It's very important you know that. I ran into him a few weeks later and told him the truth. I told him I was pregnant. I knew he was the father because we knew my husband was unlikely to father any kids."

She smiled a watery smile. "There was a chance he could, a very small chance. If it happened once it wasn't likely to happen again. So he thought he'd had his one hit and was very happy. But when Lucy was born, she had Frank's eyes. And nose. And no one in our families had hair that dark. Nothing my husband really noticed, you know. He swore she had the Brooks nose, for example. That was fine with me. And he adored her. She healed our marriage. Hugh started spending more time at home. I don't think he ever suspected she wasn't his."

Jeanine raised her chin and met Maggie's gaze squarely. "Hugh has no idea of my infidelity. I can't be too sorry. Frank gave us Lucy." Her voice broke. "And now she's gone. I'm sorry you never had the chance to know her. But you never could, don't you see? You never could, because it would have destroyed my marriage and our family."

Sorrow filled Maggie. So many secrets. In the end, she and Lucy were the ones who were cheated. Still... She finally found her voice. "Did you ask my father not to say anything?"

Jeanine bit her lip. "I did. By that time he'd met your mom. It benefited both of us to do it my way."

Maggie felt a little sick her father had let her sister go that easy.

Jeanine seemed to read her mind. "Don't think less of Frank," she said softly. "He was young, too. Madly in love with your mom. I saw them together a couple of times. He wasn't ready to be a dad at that time. People grow and change, Maggie. Remember that. I look at it as he gave my husband and me an incredible gift."

At what cost? Maybe if her father had let her mother in on the whole thing years ago, Maggie wouldn't be in this situation now. Those choices were on her father, even if Maggie and her mother were paying the price.

"I don't know what to say," Maggie admitted. While she'd known the very bare bones of the story, she hadn't been prepared for the whole thing. "I'm feeling a little overwhelmed right now."

Jeanine laid her hands flat on the table, her eyes sad. "Of course you are. This is a story that played out more than thirty years ago, but to you it's brand-new."

Tears pricked Maggie's eyes and she could only nod.

Jeanine reached into her purse, pulled out an envelope and slid it across the table. "These are copies of some of Lucy's pictures. You have the right to know a bit about her, even if it never happened that you could meet in person. I'm sorry for that. I truly am."

Maggie took the envelope, felt its heft in her hand. The story of a woman—her sister—in her hand. She did not open it, instead slid into her own purse.

When Jeanine spoke again, her words were whispered. "Can you—can you tell me how Cody is?"

Chapter Twelve

Maggie's head came up in shock. "Why do you think I know?"

Jeanine closed her eyes. "I know you're his nanny. A woman I know in town told me."

Maggie recoiled. How did she handle this? And who knew who she was?

"I know all about secrets, Maggie," Jeanine reminded her with a sad smile. "Yours is safe with me. The woman I know doesn't know who you are. I will say my daughter was very unhappy in her marriage. Some of that was her personality—she was very impulsive and I don't think they were ever really suited. A lot of it is on Josh. He wasn't there for her."

Maggie caught the thread of bitterness and tried to reconcile Jeanine's words with the Josh she knew. "I'm sorry to hear that," she said finally. She thought of Josh's banked anger at this woman and her husband. "I'm not comfortable sharing anything about Cody. But I can say Josh is a wonderful father to Cody and he's a very happy little boy."

Jeanine nodded. "I understand. I just…wanted to know."

Impulsively Maggie reached across the table and squeezed her hand. "You can call him," she suggested. "Work it out. See Cody."

Jeanine's eyes brimmed with tears. "It's not that easy.

We exchanged terrible words." Maggie saw her shudder. "Terrible words," she repeated softly.

"I'm so sorry to hear that," Maggie murmured. Cody was the loser in this game but it wasn't her place to point that out to this woman. Her heart ached for all of them.

Jeanine opened her wallet and pulled out a ten. "Here. Pay the bill with this. I can't stay. I just…can't. I'm so very sorry, Maggie, that you never knew my girl, never could know her. She was a wonderful person. You would have loved her."

Jeanine stood and looked at Maggie, regret etching her features. "And I think she would have loved you."

Maggie sat very still as Jeanine left, emotions roiling in her heart. It all made sense now. Jeanine's refusal to see her. What if Maggie resembled Lucy? How could she explain Maggie? What would it do to her husband and marriage if he knew the daughter he'd adored was not his? And really, if Josh let Maggie stay around, how could they have a relationship with Cody? Jeanine would need to come clean with her husband. It seemed Maggie had inadvertently forced the other woman's hand. But the choice Jeanine had to make wasn't on Maggie.

Tears burned in her throat, and she forced them down. She needed to talk to Kerry.

She paid the bill and left the restaurant with the precious envelope of pictures tucked in her purse. She would look at them at home, in the privacy of her own room.

As soon as she got in her car, she called Kerry. Her friend answered on the second ring.

"I met Lucy's mom today," she said without preamble.

She heard Kerry's indrawn breath. "After she refused to see you?"

Maggie leaned her head back on the seat. "Yeah." She filled her friend in on the details of the meeting.

"Wow," Kerry said softly. "Just—wow."

"I know. I don't know if I feel any better," Maggie murmured.

"But now you know about her. You learned a lot. It must at least partly explain why your father did what he did. It's not easy to learn about a sister after you've already lost her."

True. "She gave me pictures." Maggie glanced at her purse. The envelope almost gave off an aura of its own.

"Did you look at them?"

"Not yet. Not here. I'll wait till I get home."

"You okay, Maggie?" Kerry's question was soft.

"I will be." It wasn't every day you learned the answer to deep family secrets. "It's a lot to take in, I guess. I'm glad I met her."

They talked for a few more minutes, then Maggie disconnected, put the phone on the passenger seat and started the car. She had a lot to process now that she knew the truth and had seen firsthand the damage of decades of secrets and lies.

She needed to put a stop to it.

Maggie hadn't looked at the pictures yet. She'd tucked them in her drawer, but was waiting for a truly private moment. So far, in the four days since she'd met Jeanine, there hadn't been many of those. Plus, every time she thought of the envelope, the mounting guilt she felt over sleeping with Josh threatened to strangle her.

Josh seemed pretty well unaffected. He'd been polite, friendly, not quite distant. Clearly he'd enjoyed their one night and was willing to leave it at that. Men. She sighed. If only she could compartmentalize half as well.

For the most part she thought she'd done pretty well in the days since their incredible night together. She hadn't attacked him again, hadn't stolen a kiss, a hug, a butt squeeze.

And in return hadn't had any of those things stolen from her, which depressed her *because* it depressed her.

Silly.

Still, once or twice she'd caught him looking at her with hunger and longing. She shivered a little at the thought. So maybe he wasn't quite as indifferent as she'd thought. It didn't make it any easier.

Cody's laugh drifted in from outside, and she snapped out of her thoughts. She'd sent him out in the backyard to play and he was attempting to make a snowman. So far he'd managed to roll a few small balls and stacked them carefully into a child-size snowman.

She opened the door to tell him what a great job he'd done when he kicked it down using his ninja moves—a bit hampered by all the snow gear—and laughed again.

She grinned. She couldn't help it. "Hey, Code, what'd that snowman do to you?"

He turned around and punched his fists in the air. "I beat the bad guy, Maggie! Did you see?"

"I sure did. Thanks for keeping us safe. Do you want to come in for cocoa?"

Cody plowed through the snow with a whoop and a few seconds later Maggie helped him out of his wet stuff. When the kitchen door opened, she spun in surprise.

"Josh! Wait, is it—" For a second she thought she'd managed to lose major track of the time. Had she wasted hours mooning over what couldn't be?

He laughed. "Don't worry, it's almost noon. I tried to call but got no answer. Today's our Christmas lunch at the clinic. I came to get Cody and see if you'd want to come, too."

"Maggie was makin' me cocoa," Cody said. "I beat the bad guy."

Josh didn't blink. "That's good, buddy."

"Come see. You can see." He tugged on Josh's hand and Maggie stepped aside to let them pass.

Her heart tugged watching the big man and the little boy look out the window. Then it squeezed when he laughed outright.

"Cody, that's fantastic. I love it. Nice job, big guy." He held out a hand for a high five, which Cody happily gave.

"So. You coming?" Josh turned to her. "It's good food. I ordered from Mack's Deli and the staff all bring dishes to pass." His eyes pleaded with her to say yes.

Weak thing that she was, she nodded. "I'd love to."

She and Cody followed Josh to the clinic. They got out of the car and met Josh in the parking lot.

"Ready?"

"I'm starved," Cody announced.

Josh's look was full of affection. "Of course you are. Lucky for you there's lots of food."

"Cookies, too?"

Maggie stifled a giggle as Josh nodded. "Of course. But real food first. Okay?"

Cody sighed. "Okay."

Maggie followed them through the doors. She could hear the laughter and the music from outside.

Nerves did a little dance in her belly. She should have stayed home, should keep her distance. Somehow, it constantly proved impossible.

Marta came right over, JT in tow. Cody lit right up at the sight of his friend.

"So glad you came," she said with a warm smile. "Eat up! We've got lots. And not much time."

Maggie took Cody's coat and laid it and her own on a chair while Josh guided Cody to the well-stocked buffet.

"He's such a good dad," Marta mused.

"I agree," Maggie said quietly.

"He's trying to be both parents," Marta said in a low tone. "That's why it's so good to see the dynamic with you and Cody. He looks up to you as a mother figure. He needs that in his life. Josh, hard as he tries, can't be both."

Mother figure. Maggie's stomach rolled. Cody asked her to be his mom. She'd never said anything to Josh. She'd hoped that Cody simply loved her in the way he loved everyone he knew.

Not that he truly looked at her as a mom. How easily she'd slid into the role.

How hard it would be to leave it.

"What a day," Josh groaned as he sank into his desk chair. They'd been packed with patients before and after the Christmas lunch. Lots of add-ons and not just the ones who wanted him to marry their daughters, either. Something seemed to be going around, and half the kids in Holden's Crossing had it.

Maggie. Josh closed his eyes for a second. More than anything, he wanted to be home, with her. Or not. His feelings ran between wanting and guilt and knowing he could never really have her.

The guilt was pretty strong. In fact, it ate at him more the stronger his feelings grew. This was twofold. One, he'd broken his promise to Lucy. No matter how he tried to deny it, he'd gotten involved with Maggie in every sense of the word. Two, he'd never have slept with her—with her wounded soul and trusting eyes—if he didn't have feelings for her, especially since she lived in the same house. He knew she wouldn't take it lightly, either.

Which didn't make any of it any easier. He'd decided to run with it, to take advantage of the brief time they'd been given. He really couldn't say what came over him, just a firm sense he needed to grab the chance if Maggie was willing.

Oh, she'd been willing.

He shut his eyes again. It'd help if he could stop flashing back to snippets of their lovemaking. Seeing her at the moment of climax as she shattered in his arms. The curve of her breast in the firelight. His blood heated at the memory.

One night only. He kept reminding himself, but he had a sneaking suspicion he'd be flashing back to that night for a long time to come.

He snagged his jacket off the coat tree in the corner of the room with more force than necessary. The tree rocked and he caught it before it fell on him. He needed to relax, to accept how things were.

Exactly as he told everyone he wanted them to be. Except he sure wasn't happy.

Everyone else had left already, except Marta, and she stuck her head in his office on her way out.

"Need anything?" she asked the way she always did. He shook his head, as much to dislodge his thoughts as to tell her no.

"All set, thanks," he said. "Actually, I'll walk out with you." He shrugged into his jacket and grabbed his case while Marta waited by the door, keys jingling in her hand.

"In a hurry?" he asked her, amused, and saw her eyes refocus.

"What? Me? No. Just thinking about all the stuff I have to do before Christmas." She held her keys still.

"It's still a couple of weeks away," he said with the

cavalier attitude only a guy could manage and thus was rewarded with a sour look.

"Uh-huh. Exactly," she said and rolled her eyes. "What are you getting Maggie for Christmas?"

Josh nearly stopped short. "I, ah, hadn't thought about it." And that was the truth. Would he be getting Maggie a present? A professional one, of course, but...a personal gift? Dismay ran through him. What was the protocol for buying a gift for someone you'd hired, who lived in your house, who you'd slept with once and from whom you wanted way more than you could ever have?

It exhausted him to even think about it.

Marta ran her gloved hand through the fluffy snow on the back of her car and shook her head. "You'd better get on it," she said.

"Why's that?" he asked carefully, not liking her tone. She sounded...reproachful. Like he was about to mess up royally. More than he already had.

She opened her door and pulled out her snow brush. "You've at least kissed her, right?" The question was so casual, asked while she swept the fluffy stuff off her car, she may as well have asked him about the weather.

Or whacked him with the brush.

His mind went blank so his mouth helpfully took over. "How can you tell?"

She sent him an amused look, propped her free hand on her hip and pointed the brush at him. "Because I know you. Because you've alternated between holy hell and mooningly sick. Not only that, but you're in love with her and scared out of your ever-loving mind, right?"

"Um." That comment led down a mine-filled path. "I'm not in love with her. I'm not in love with anyone." Denial, panic and a low, deep-down knowledge she might be right. *Hell.* He shook it off. She couldn't be right.

Marta shook her head and tossed the snowy brush on the floor of the backseat. "I hope that's not the case. Get her a gorgeous gift for Christmas, Josh. Show her you love her."

Gorgeous gift, he could probably handle. Show her he loved her? Well, he didn't. So that wasn't possible.

"We'll see," he said finally. "But Marta, I'm not in love with her."

Marta regarded him for a moment before slipping in her car, her gaze sad. "That's too bad, doc. Because I'd say she's sure in love with you." She closed the door on that little bomb and left him standing in the snow, stunned. Maggie, in love with him?

He couldn't answer that, didn't know what he wanted the answer to be.

Could he love her?

That was a different story. Yes, he could. Absolutely. If he were able. If she wanted it. If he could be sure he'd be a better husband this time around than he'd managed to be to Lucy.

None of those were absolute, and every one represented a risk he didn't know if he was capable of taking, because he did not want to hurt Maggie. Or Cody. Or, okay, himself.

He quickly swiped the snow off the SUV as more sifted down around him. He shoved all thoughts of love and Maggie out of the way as he climbed in his vehicle. He wasn't going there right now, or ever if he could help it. What he and Maggie shared had been hot and wonderful and hell, yes, he'd do it again in a heartbeat but that didn't mean he loved her.

Right?

Josh did an admirable job of cramming all his feelings back in that increasingly too-small box, like trying to close the suitcases Lucy used to pack before a weekend getaway. Back when they'd been able to stand each other long enough to actually do a weekend getaway. Which had been…probably only the first couple of months of dating.

Sadness washed over him. That should have been a big clue to their lack of compatibility. But all bets were off once Lucy realized she was pregnant. He'd wanted to do right by her, by their baby. He'd insisted they marry. She'd been more hesitant.

What if he'd listened to her? Would she be here today? Would she like Maggie?

He shook off the thoughts. That way lay craziness and he still wouldn't have the answer.

Now, he sat on the couch in front of the fire, reading Cody a book about talking trains on an island while the Christmas tree glowed and the fire crackled. Maggie had left to run errands. He had one ear tuned to the garage, waiting for her car to pull in because then he could relax all the way because she'd be home.

He told himself he'd worry about anyone out in the snow, not just Maggie. That funny ache under his heart? Indigestion. Not him missing her when she was gone. Not him feeling panicky because the roads were iffy.

Josh closed the book and handed it to Cody. "Here you go. Brush your teeth and I'll be right up to tuck you in."

Cody traipsed upstairs, book in one hand, worn-out bear in the other, talking to the bear about the trains. Josh stared into the flames for a few minutes, which was probably why he jumped a mile when Cody sidled up to him and spoke, his eyes serious.

"Daddy? Can Maggie be my new mommy?"

Josh's heart came to a full stop. Of all the things Cody could have hit him with, this wasn't even on the list. He cleared his throat. "Well, Cody, you know you have a mommy. In Heaven." They'd been over this but he knew it was a concept out of a four-year-old's grasp.

Cody frowned. "But I want one here. With me. Who can play with me. Like Maggie."

Josh couldn't help himself. "You think Maggie would make a good mom?"

Cody nodded. "She smells good an' plays with me an' makes you smile. I *love* her."

Josh's heart cracked as he pulled his earnest small son into his embrace. If only it were that easy to insert Maggie in their lives. He didn't know how to do it without shoving Lucy to the side. Or opening them both up to more heartbreak.

"I like her, too." *A lot. More than I should.* He couldn't use the other *L* word. He was worried he'd gone beyond mere *like*. "But you need more than liking someone for a mom."

Cody nodded. "She said that, too."

Josh froze. "You asked her about this?" He was afraid to ask what she'd said.

"Yep." He twisted to look up at him. "She said it wasn't like gettin' a puppy." He frowned. "But I don't want a puppy. I want a new mom."

"You don't need a mommy, Code. You have me." He offered a smile, but saw, by the reproach and tears in Cody's eyes, he'd missed the mark by a country mile.

"I want a mom," Cody said stubbornly. "I want Maggie. I know!" He brightened. "Maggie said we could go talk to Santa. I'll ask him!"

Josh blanched. Uh-oh. "Santa doesn't bring that sort of thing for gifts. He brings, you know, presents. Boxes. Things he can carry in his sleigh. In his bag. Not actual people."

"Maggie's already here, so he wouldn't have to bring

her," Cody pointed out and in spite of himself Josh nearly chuckled. Kid was sharp.

"You're right, she is. But Santa can't make people love each other or be parents. That's not fair to them. What if they don't want to be a parent?"

Cody looked at him in horror. "You don't think Maggie will want to be my mom?"

Josh shut his eyes. How else could he mess this up? "No. That's not what I meant. I don't know if she would. She'd be a good mom, I think. I just meant Santa can't make someone be a mom or dad."

Cody's shoulders slumped and tears slid out of his eyes. Josh's own started to burn. Then Cody straightened. "I don't believe you. I'm going to ask him." Clearly cheered at this conclusion, Cody wiped his eyes and smiled at him a little defiantly.

Hell. "Just to be safe, why don't you think of other things you want? Don't you have a Christmas list? I bet Santa will try really hard to bring you what you want." Still, he knew it wouldn't take the place of a mother figure in Cody's life. The thought left him hollow and wrecked inside. He stood and lifted Cody with him, trying to sound normal. "Let's go get you tucked in, okay?"

After getting Cody settled, he sat down on his bed heavily. The whole conversation, on top of Marta's observations from earlier, had him in knots. The mommy thing needed to be addressed soon. Cody had attached to Maggie in a completely different way than his previous nanny, and Josh had no clue how to navigate the waters now. Asking Maggie was clearly out of the question.

Since asking her might mean you have to admit how you feel?

It wasn't her problem. He'd deal with it.

Headlights played over the wall, and he heard the garage door go up. Relief slipped through him, and he was too emotionally exhausted to stop it.

Maggie. Back, at last, from her errands.

He thought about going down to meet her, but after Cody's bombshell his emotions were too raw and too close to the surface. So instead, he closed his door all the way, rare for him this early, but he needed the barrier.

He heard her come up the stairs, even though her step was light. He was so attuned to her, it was like he was right there beside her, part of her shadow. She went right past his door, plastic bags rustling. Was that a pause in her footsteps? Or his hopeful imagination? He heard her door open, then close.

Safe. He whooshed out a breath, then almost laughed.

From what? The thought was absurd. Maybe she was the one who was safe from him dragging her into his lair. Or his bed. Or hell, the shower he was about to take. A tightening in his nether regions told him which way his body voted.

With a groan, he went into the bathroom and turned the water setting to cold—again—and forced himself to think about shoveling snow.

Chapter Thirteen

Maggie dumped the shopping bags on the floor. Since both Josh and Cody were in bed, it seemed like the perfect opportunity to look at the pictures Jeanine had given her. She pulled the envelope out of her underwear drawer with slightly shaking hands.

She sat cross-legged on her bed, took a deep breath and slid the photos out. There were more than a dozen of them. She fumbled a little as she spread them out, her eyes already stinging.

Oh. *Oh.* She lost her breath.

Lucy as a laughing toddler in a little wading pool, wearing a ruffly pink bathing suit. Lucy as a proud kindergartner, barrettes in her dark hair, leaning on the man who must be her father. Lucy as a little girl of maybe nine, arms around the neck of a happily panting yellow Lab. Lucy as a young teen in her soccer uniform, braces glinting on her teeth, grin wide as she helped hoist a huge trophy. Lucy at prom. Maggie's jaw dropped—the navy strapless gown Lucy wore was very similar to the one she herself had worn a couple of years later. Lucy at graduation—both high school and college—smiling into the camera, arms around her beaming parents. Still others of birthdays, camping, general goofiness.

Tears slid unchecked down Maggie's face. She couldn't comprehend the loss of this girl, of Jeanine and Hugh's little girl. All along, she'd been thinking of Lucy in terms of being her sister, Cody's mom. Her father's unknown daughter. Not as a girl and woman who was loved and cherished and missed beyond life itself. These pictures told a very brief, poignant tale of a beloved daughter.

A gift, Jeanine had called Lucy. From Maggie's father. If only her own mother could see what Lucy had meant to this other family, maybe she'd release some of her pain and anger.

She carefully shuffled the pictures back into the envelope and lay back on her pillows with them on her heart. She couldn't fix what had happened, but she thought she understood a little better why her father honored Jeanine's request to be left alone. He hadn't loved her any more than she loved him. But he'd seen how much Jeanine would love the baby and what it meant to her to have this chance to mend her marriage.

She preferred to think of it as a selfless act, even if misguided, rather than a selfish one. She sat up and slid the envelope onto her bedside table. She'd tell Josh the whole story right after Christmas. She'd find the right words and hope he forgave her and understood what she'd been trying to do.

The knot in her stomach eased a bit.

Then she rolled on her side and fell asleep, into vivid dreams of a ponytailed, laughing girl who looked an awful lot like Lucy.

The next evening was dinner at Ellen's. Maggie went because it was important to Cody. She and Josh were, as ever, polite to each other. Clearly, though, Ellen picked up on vibes she didn't like because she kept frowning in Josh's direction.

He pretended not to notice.

She had to leave soon after eating to meet Hannah, so she helped clear the table. Ellen caught her in the kitchen, her gaze direct.

"Is anything going on with you and Josh?"

"Um." Maggie set the glasses she'd been carrying down before she dropped them. "No."

The other woman muttered something Maggie didn't quite catch, but she'd swear it included something like "stupid boy." The look Ellen arrowed at Josh made Maggie step back.

At some point she'd have to tell Ellen it wouldn't work. Make sure she really heard. But not today.

She made her escape with a hug for Cody and a "see ya" for Josh.

Ellen looked to be on the warpath. She almost pitied Josh. Almost.

His mother appeared back in the dining room.

"Young man," Ellen said, her voice stern, "we need to talk."

Cody looked up, confused, as Josh got to his feet. He'd known this was coming. "What'd I do?" Cody asked and Ellen laughed.

"Sorry, sweetie. Not you. You can watch a movie and play with your cars and trains, okay?"

Josh settled Cody in then met his mother in the kitchen, where she handed him a cup of coffee with a frown.

"Are you trying to run that lovely young lady off?" she demanded. "My goodness, Joshua, what did you do to her?"

Josh closed his eyes and took a sip of the coffee. It'd be decaf, of course. "Nothing, Mom." Images of them in bed flashed through his head. Well, nothing he could tell her about, anyway. "We just— We're having some problems connecting." Hell. How many ways were there to say lame?

Ellen's brow shot up. "You are in love with her and all you can say is you're having trouble connecting?"

Josh blanched. "What? How—?" That was the second person who'd made the same observation. He still didn't want to believe it.

Ellen rolled her eyes and set her mug on the counter with a thunk. "I have eyes. And I know you. Better than you do, apparently." She shook her finger at him. "Don't screw this up. It's your second chance. Why would you let it go?"

"Um, because I didn't do so well with the first one?" he shot back, then stopped, stunned at what he'd admitted. He'd never told his mother what a failure he'd been at marriage.

"I know," she said softly. "I know. But did it ever occur to you that marriage takes two? How hard did Lucy work at it, Josh? Why would you take all the blame for something that as far as I can tell is two-sided?"

Had it been two-sided? Josh couldn't remember. He'd taken the blame for the whole mess for so long he honestly couldn't tell what had really happened and what he'd just accepted as the truth.

"If you love her," Ellen said softly, "you'd better get out there and prove it. She needs you to prove it. And maybe you need it, too." She gave him a hug, then held him at arm's length. "I know, I'm your mom, but I want you to be happy. Maggie does that to you. Please let her in."

Josh shook his head. There was more to the story than she knew. Not to mention it wasn't easy to let go of years of guilt.

Maybe that's because you don't really want to, whispered a little voice in his head. Josh forced that thought right back down wherever it came from. Of course he wanted to get over it. He just knew he never would.

"Talk to her," Ellen ordered, and Josh snapped back to the present. "Work this out. For God's sake give it a chance. For your sake. For Cody's sake," she added softly, and Josh closed his eyes.

"I can't just give him a new mom," he said, wondering why all this was so clear to him yet no one else seemed to get it. "It's not that easy."

Ellen sighed and picked up her mug again. "It's not about replacing Lucy, dear. She'll always be Cody's mom. You're not going to take her away from Cody by marrying another woman. You'll be teaching Cody how to love. What's he going to think, growing up with only you?"

What's wrong with that? he wanted to ask. *Why can't I be both parents?* But he didn't. He didn't really want to hear the answer.

Ellen watched him place his mug in the sink. "Promise me you'll talk to her," she said. "I don't want to pry but I really like Maggie. Cody adores her. And you need her."

Josh sighed. "I'll give it a shot." Someday. Maybe.

"Just try. If it's not going to work you need to know you did all you could."

Right. Josh headed out to his SUV with Cody. His mother's words rang in his ears. First things first. He needed to deal with Cody wanting Maggie for his mom. Tomorrow he was supposed to take Cody to see Santa at the town's Christmas festival. He needed to talk Cody into a new wish. One he could buy in a store. And wrap. And put under the damn tree. The rest could wait.

Chicken.

No. He was being smart and safe. Someday Cody would understand.

* * *

"You ready for this?" Maggie asked Cody as they stood in line at the band shell in the park to see Santa. She tried not to remember that Josh had kissed her right over there, under one of the trees the magical night they'd spent together. Now the park was full of people, ice skaters, children and parents, all taking part in Holden's Crossing's annual Christmas-at-the-lake festival.

Cody danced in place. "Yep." He didn't seem too disturbed his dad wasn't there. Josh couldn't make it at the last minute—he'd been needed at the hospital, so Maggie brought Cody down here by herself.

Just as well. No more false family outings. Plus, she treasured the opportunity to share this with Cody.

The line for Santa was deep, but thanks to the fact Cody knew the little girl in front of them from swim class, he was entertained. The girl's parents were nice and Maggie passed the half hour in pleasant conversation with them. It was nice to talk with someone who wasn't trying to fix her up with Josh.

When it was the little girl's turn, Cody examined the process carefully.

"I think he's real," he stage-whispered, and Maggie smiled down at him.

"Do you? Why is that?"

"He looks real," Cody said, and Maggie had to agree. The man's hair and beard were clearly natural. "I need the real Santa for my wish."

Before Maggie could ask exactly what that meant, the little girl in front was finished and it was Cody's turn. Maggie urged him forward and watched as he climbed on Santa's knee.

"What brings you and your mom out today?" Santa

asked kindly, and Maggie sucked in a breath. Cody looked at him intently.

"She's not my mom." He glanced at Maggie, then lowered his voice. "But that's what I want for Christmas. Maggie for my mom."

The world spun as Maggie met Santa's eyes over Cody's head. The compassion in them nearly undid her. "You do? That's not generally the kind of thing I can bring you, son."

Cody smiled up at him, a smile of absolute faith that had Maggie's eyes burning. "That's what my daddy said, too. But, see, that's okay. She already lives with us. She's my nanny. So you don't have to bring her. You just have to help her love us."

Maggie pressed her hand to her mouth. *Help her love us.* If he only knew. She'd give just about anything to tell him how much she loved both of them.

How badly she wanted to stay.

Santa looked at Maggie, then nodded and looked directly into Cody's eyes. "I can't promise you, son. But I can tell you this is a season for miracles."

Cody nodded sagely. "An' that's what I need."

Santa redirected him to mention a toy but Cody was steadfast in his wish. When he slipped off Santa's lap, Santa met Maggie's gaze and gestured her over.

"Is there any hope for his wish?" he asked quietly while Cody was distracted by an elf with a candy cane.

Maggie bit her lip. If only it was this simple to fix it, to tell Santa it was her dearest wish, too. But circumstances being what they were… She forced herself to meet his gaze. The sympathy in Santa's eyes nearly undid her. "It's not that simple, I'm afraid. If it was—" She trailed off. If it were, they'd be a family. Ironically, she'd managed to make it impossible for that to happen.

"Like I told him, it's a season for miracles," he murmured and patted her hand. "Never underestimate what the heart wants, my dear. Merry Christmas."

"Merry Christmas," she whispered and turned away before she burst into tears in front of practically the entire town. Forcing the sorrow down, she hurried to catch Cody, her heart aching. Josh would ask what Cody wanted. What would she tell him? How could she tell him?

Cody chattered excitedly as they made their way to the food booths. "I hope I get it, Maggie. I know Santa can do it," he said confidently, and tears stung her eyes.

"Can you tell me what toy you asked for?" she asked, noticing for the first time the dark clouds on the horizon. Snow was on the way but it wasn't supposed to arrive till the evening.

Cody named a Lego set then added, "But I can't tell you my real wish. It's a secret."

Maggie rested her gloved hand on Cody's head. What a mess this would be when it didn't turn out the way he wanted. Was there any way to avoid heartbreak now? Josh needed to know about the wish and talk to Cody. The little boy clearly had his hopes pinned on them being a couple— no doubt he could pick up on the vibes between them, even if he thankfully didn't know what they meant.

She ordered and paid for two hot chocolates and one elephant ear and they went to sit on a picnic table that had been brushed off. All around them families played and laughed and Maggie was acutely aware of what Cody didn't have and what he wanted. A mom. It wouldn't be her, and it wasn't in her power to fix that hole in his life.

But it was in Josh's.

She frowned at the thought. When would he realize that his self-imposed exile was hurting Cody? After she left, would it be easier for him to move on? The thought made her feel ill and she swallowed hard.

"Daddy!" The joy in Cody's voice rang out. Maggie lifted her head to see Josh striding toward them through the park, still in scrubs. Her pulse tripped, and she pulled a napkin out of her parka pocket with slightly shaking hands.

"Cody, let's wipe the sugar off your face," she said with a laugh as Josh reached them.

"At least I'm in time for the elephant ear," he said as he sat down opposite them. She pushed the plate across the table to him. "Did you see Santa, Code?"

Maggie held her breath as Cody nodded. Before he could say anything else, another family stopped to say hello to Josh and Cody and the subject was dropped.

As she watched them, a little shiver ran though her that had nothing to do with the cold. All she wanted, all she needed, was right here at this table in the cold, laughing over a sticky elephant ear. Josh's laugh hit her in places completely inappropriate for a family function. When their gazes met, she saw the same desire in his eyes, too, and realized she was in way over her head.

"I think I'll head home," she said casually. Cody shook his head.

"Daddy just got here," he protested.

Maggie slipped her arm around him and squeezed lightly. "No, honey. I didn't mean you have to leave. You and your dad stay. I'll head out." *Before I get in any deeper.*

"Stay," Josh said quietly and with that word, when she looked at him, everything crashed around her, all the emotions she'd been battling for so long, and she knew, in a crystal-clear moment of clarity, how very, very lost she was.

She was in love with him. Completely, absolutely, down-to-the-bottom-of-her-soul in love with the man.

How could she have let this happen? She knew better, but somehow her heart had gotten away from her.

"Maggie? Is everything all right? You look a little pale all of a sudden." Josh stood next to her, the concern on his face nearly undoing her.

"Oh, I'm fine. Just a little too much elephant ear, I guess," she said, summoning a smile. It must have worked, because he stepped back.

"Are you gonna stay?" Looking at Cody's anxious face, turned up to her, crusted in sugar, made her heart melt. She was in this so far there was no good way out.

"I'll stay for a bit," she agreed.

Josh didn't know he was holding his breath until Maggie assented. He let it out slowly and Cody gave a little cheer.

"Can we go skating?" he asked. "I really wanna. Please?"

Josh hesitated. Skating—and hockey—was something he'd given up after Lucy's death. It didn't seem right to deny Cody, though, just because his dad had issues. "Sure. We can give it a try."

They threw away their garbage and headed for the rink. The lake wasn't quite smooth enough for skating yet, but the rink the park made every year was ready to go and full of skaters. It took a few minutes to get set and he was pleased and surprised to see Maggie glide effortlessly on the ice.

"You skate," he said, and she smiled and did a little spin.

"I do. It's been a few years, though." She reached for Cody's hand. "Want to go around with me?"

The little boy clutched her hand and they made their way around the rink, Cody slowly getting the proper gliding motion. Josh made a few laps himself, exchanging greetings with other skaters, some of whom were his old hockey buddies.

It felt good to be back on skates. He'd missed it.

Across the rink, some teenagers were showing off, skating backward far too fast. Before Josh could holler a warning, they'd crashed right into Maggie and Cody, who dropped like rocks.

Horror pounded through Josh as he skated toward the heap of people, looking frantically for Cody and Maggie. She'd taken the brunt of the fall, he saw when he got close enough. The older kids were removing themselves from the heap and he could hear their apologies as he approached. Maggie was sitting up and Cody looked stunned when Josh got to them.

"Are you all right?" He pulled Cody into his chest and tugged off his glove to palm Maggie's face, right there in front of God and the whole damn town.

He didn't care.

Her cheeks were pink and cold under his touch and his gaze dropped to her mouth. Cody wiggled in his arms.

"I'm okay," he said. "Maggie caught me."

She caught me, too. The thought stunned him for a heartbeat as he stared into the blue eyes of the woman who'd captured his heart.

Marta had been right. He'd never hear the end of it now. He didn't care.

She frowned, a worried look on her face. "Josh?"

He shook off the thought as he got to his feet, offering his hand to Maggie, too. She moved gingerly toward the benches, and he sat down with her, not caring if his thigh touched hers. "You okay?"

"I… Yeah. Just sore. I'd forgotten how much it hurts to hit the ice," she said, rubbing her knee with a wince.

He touched her knee gently, sure he could feel the heat of her skin through her jeans. Cody sat next to him, kicking his feet. "Do you need me to look at it?"

Her gaze skittered to his, then away. "Oh, no. It's just a bruise." She leaned around him to smile at Cody, and the movement brought her breasts in contact with his arm. He was aware of it even through their coats. "Guess we took quite a spill, huh?"

"Yeah," he agreed. "I don't think I like it much."

Maggie laughed. "Falling is scary. But the rest of the time, skating is fun."

Falling is scary. Ain't that the truth. Uncharted territory for him. "We should go," he said, bending over to unlace Cody's skates.

"But we just got here," Cody protested. "I don't want to go."

"You've been here a while, Code. We can come back and skate another time," he said. "When it's not so busy." It'd been a mistake to try this. Cody had gotten hurt, and so had Maggie. Granted, both were minor injuries only, but it scared him how much worse it could have been. Not only had he failed to protect Lucy's son, but he'd also fallen in love with the nanny.

With Maggie.

Part of him wanted to shout it from the rooftops but he knew she wouldn't want to hear it. They walked to his car at a slower pace than usual. Since Cody and Maggie had walked, it was a good thing he'd driven. He hadn't counted on injuries.

When they got home, Maggie excused herself to go take a bath to soak her sore body. Josh tried not to listen to the water running and when he walked by her room the faint scent of bath salts tickled his nose. He tried not to picture her naked in the water and what he so badly wanted to do to her. With her.

And failed.

He was so damn screwed.

He took a deep breath and concentrated on Cody, who was bouncing around.

"Code, what did you ask Santa for?" he asked, hoping

to hear a nice toy. Hoping he'd listened to Josh and let go of his wish for Maggie and a mom.

Cody sent him a cagey look. "Nothing."

Or not. Josh's heart sank. "Nothing? At all? You waited in line all that time for nothing?"

Cody gave him a little smile and shook his head.

Now he knew. His heart broke. "Cody, we talked about this. Santa can't bring you a mom."

"He was real, Daddy," Cody said simply. "An' Maggie's here."

Josh stood in the middle of the living room and stared at the tree, sick with the knowledge he couldn't possibly produce the one thing his boy wanted most for Christmas.

Even though he wanted it, too.

Chapter Fourteen

Maggie walked past Josh's bedroom door and saw him looking at a pile of gifts on the floor.

She stopped. She couldn't help herself. "Taking a bit of chance, aren't you?"

He looked up quickly. "Maggie. Yeah, I guess so. I need to start wrapping but..." He looked back at the pile. "There's so much to do."

She hesitated. What the heck. "I can help," she offered. "I love to wrap."

He looked so relieved, it was almost comical. "Really? You'd do that?"

"Sure. You've got paper?"

He walked to the closet and Maggie did not focus on his delicious backside as he moved away. She forced her attention to the presents on the floor and tried not to remember how intimate they'd gotten. How he'd loved her, how she'd responded. Her body fired up in response.

She blinked. Blushed. *Whoa*. This wouldn't work.

Hoping he wouldn't notice her little lapse into fantasy land, she busied herself sorting the toys into little piles by size.

"Here we go," he said and thumped a plastic tub in front of her. It was half-full of paper and ribbon and bows.

"Very nice," Maggie said as he pried the top off. "So where do we start?"

Josh sighed. "Anywhere."

Biting back a grin, Maggie picked up a box, then selected a roll of paper.

"What?" Josh looked put out.

She gave in and laughed. "You. You act like this is such a chore but you'll do it anyway."

"Ah. Well. I've never been much of a wrapper."

They worked in relative quiet, the TV on low in the background. *It's a Wonderful Life* played, and the stack of wrapped gifts grew. Maggie treasured these moments as they worked in companionable silence, just the snip of scissors and the crinkle of paper to punctuate the movie in the background.

She realized Josh had stopped working and was watching her play with a fancy bow. She frowned at him, then at the package. "What?"

"He'll just rip that off, Maggie." There was quiet amusement in his voice.

She shrugged. Of course he would. "That's not the point. I like to do it."

He took the merrily wrapped gift from her and his hands brushed hers. She sucked in a breath, feeling the mood go from companionable with manageable undercurrents, to something…more. Something decadent and dangerous.

Her breath shortened as he looked at her, intense in the flickering light of the television. He picked up a roll of curling ribbon and spun it out a few inches. "Tell me," he said, his voice low, "I'm not the only one imagining new uses for this stuff."

Her mouth went dry. It was the first real reference he'd made to their one night of lovemaking. They'd been good about skirting the subject. A lot of subjects.

She found her voice. "Um, no. Trust me. You're not."

She met his gaze, saw the pain and the wanting there, but couldn't get a single word out. He held out his hand and she crossed the pile of gifts to settle on his lap, her legs around his waist, and felt the hard ridge of his erection against her core. With a groan, he crushed his mouth on hers, and she fell into the kiss like it was the only thing keeping her alive.

He pulled away to nibble on her neck, then slid his hands under her shirt to run his thumbs over her nipples, which pushed against the rough lace of her bra. Her brain tried to kick on, albeit fuzzily. She needed to pull away. She was not going down this road, not until she told him... Oh. He'd pushed up her shirt and was teasing at her nipples with his teeth and lips and tongue and her thoughts scattered again.

She pulled his head back to her and met him in a crushing kiss then managed, barely, to pull away. It wasn't right to take this anywhere, no matter how badly she wanted to. She saw the regret in his eyes as she pulled back and climbed off his lap. "Sorry," he murmured. "I'm having a hard time keeping my hands and mouth to myself."

"Oh, me, too," she breathed, and a slow grin quirked the edges of his mouth.

"Really?"

What the heck. "Really. But—" she settled opposite him again and tried to calm her racing heart "—we have work to do."

He shook his head slightly as if to clear it. "Right. Work." Then he looked at her again, like she was dessert and he was in dire need of something sweet and she nearly forgot everything that had been left unsaid.

"Josh." His name was a croak.

He cleared his throat. "Yeah?"

She wanted to tell him not to look at her, not to make

her feel things for him that were only going to mess things up more, but those words wouldn't come. "I think you're okay without me now. We've made progress. I'm just going to go to bed."

She stood up and walked out before he could say anything to convince her to stay.

Hell. He'd gotten damn good at screwing this up but not this time. He stood up and caught up with her before she shut her bedroom door.

"We need to talk. Please," he added.

Her big blue eyes widened and something that looked like guilt flickered in their depths. "About what?"

He never thought he'd say it. "Us."

Her gaze dropped, but she stepped aside. "There is no us," she said warily.

The words, after the intimacy they'd shared just a few minutes before, physically hurt. He gestured between them. "This is all one-sided?"

In the low light he could see her blush. "No. Of course not. But 'us' implies more than…that."

He took a deep breath. "What if I want more than sex?"

Her gaze shot to his and he saw panic flash there. "What?"

He moved a little closer, hoping she couldn't see how damn scared he was. "I want more than that, Maggie. I want it all, with you." Lucy, his failed marriage, his promise to her, all flashed before him. Cody's wish. Too much on the line for this to go wrong. But he needed her. "I want to give it a shot."

Maggie sank down on the bed, looking rather shell-shocked. His gut tightened. This wasn't the response he'd hoped for. He heard her take a deep breath. "Josh. There's something you need to know."

He wanted to reassure her. "I know—I know things went badly with your ex-husband. But I'm not him, Maggie."

Sadness crossed her face and for the first time he wondered— "Oh, God. Are you still in love with him?" The thought made him sick. Could he have read the situation that wrong?

She shook her head vehemently. "Oh, no. No, I'm not. I'm not sure I ever was. It's just—" She stopped, swallowed hard.

"It's just what?" He squatted in front of her and knocked something off her bedside table. He saw her face turn stark white and heard her sharp inhale before he looked down.

Lucy's face stared up at him.

Shock coursed through him. He reached down and picked up the envelope with a shaking hand, saw his mother-in-law's neat handwriting inscribed on the front. More pictures inside. The blood roared in his ears and it was a long moment before he could breathe, let alone speak. "Why do you have pictures of Lucy?" The words rasped out of his throat.

She lifted her head and met his gaze straight on, tears shimmering in her eyes. "Because Lucy was my sister."

Poleaxed, Josh could only stare at her. "What did you say?" He couldn't have heard her right. Lucy didn't have a sister. She was an only child. It was part of the complex he'd developed—he'd had a hand in the loss of his in-laws' only child. What kind of nasty trick of fate was this?

Her hands were clasped so tightly in her lap her knuckles were white. "Lucy was my sister. Half sister," she amended. "Jeanine and my dad apparently had a one-night stand during a rough spot in her marriage. She never told her husband. As far as he knew, Lucy was his biological daughter." Her words were measured, but he caught the underpinnings of pain bracing them.

Everything clicked into place, right down to the similar color of Maggie and Cody's eyes. There was a reason he'd thought she resembled Lucy slightly. He'd put it down to the combo of dark hair and blue eyes. Now he could see it more clearly. He didn't know what to think, what to feel, other than an odd mix of emptyness and betrayal.

He wanted to feel nothing.

"So you're not here on a coincidence," he said finally, and Maggie shook her head. "You knew who we were."

She drew in a ragged breath. "I knew who Cody was, yes. I wanted to get to know him. I needed to see if I could learn anything about Lucy. But Jeanine wouldn't talk to me at the time, so—" Her voice trailed off.

"So you lied and faked your way into our lives," Josh said, amazed his voice sounded so calm as devastation took hold in his heart.

Maggie gasped and her head snapped back as if the slap had been physical, not verbal. "I never—"

"You did." Josh tried to summon the anger and ignored the pain. He'd need it to get through this. "You misrepresented yourself. If you'd been honest—"

"If I'd been honest you may not have let me in," she cried, then pressed her hands to her face for a moment. Then she dropped them and looked at him. "I just wanted to get to know Cody, be in his life, but not in a way that might open any old wounds for either of you. And I—I didn't know if you'd let me meet him."

He refused to be moved by the plea in her voice, or the truth in her words. It didn't matter what her intentions were, she hadn't been honest. And worse, she was Lucy's sister.

Sister. Could this get any more surreal?

When he opened his mouth to speak, she held up a hand. "Please let me finish. I need you to understand. I had this all planned out. I'd get to know Cody, spend some time with him, learn a little about my sister. At some point, I'd tell you my connection."

"And when was that going to be?" he asked a little bitterly. Before or after he'd lost his heart to her? Hell. "You didn't think I deserved to know from the beginning?"

She stared into the fire. "Of course you did. And once things started...happening with you and me, I knew it was going to have to be sooner rather than later. But it just—it just kept going. The time was never right."

He gave a sharp laugh. "*The right time* was when I interviewed you."

She winced. "I know." She met his gaze squarely, and he saw pain and regret there. "I'm sorry it went so far. I truly am. I should have been up front with you from the beginning but I couldn't risk the rejection—I'd lost my dad, my marriage and, for all intents and purposes, my mom. I thought this was the safest way for all of us. And I was wrong. I know it's not enough, but I'm so sorry."

Too little, way too late.

He stalked over to the French doors and looked out over the backyard, where a light snow fell steadily. "Just curious. Why did you think this was safe?"

She was quiet for a minute, but he didn't turn around to see what she was doing. "My father is gone. My mother isn't speaking to me. This was a chance to get to know part of my family I'd been missing. I needed the connection. Plus, Lucy was your wife. You loved her. I didn't want to shock you."

"I did not love my wife." The truth was out before Josh could stop it. The razor pain of the truth, of the waste of Lucy's life, sliced on his soul.

He heard Maggie gasp, felt her cross the carpet toward him. He shook his head, and she stopped. "Josh—"

The words ripped from Josh's throat as his voice rose. "I never loved her. She certainly didn't love me. We came together in flames and went down the same way. We married because she was pregnant. If she hadn't died—" He faltered. "If she hadn't died, we'd have divorced anyway. She'd already started proceedings. Because I never stopped to consider what she might want, might need. I was too wrapped up in my career. I was an awful husband to her."

He'd said it. Finally. Admitted out loud what a failure he'd been as a husband.

How ironic it had to be to Lucy's sister. The woman he'd fallen in love with.

The woman who'd betrayed him.

He turned and saw her in the middle of the room, sympathy and sorrow on her face, tears in her eyes. "Oh, Josh."

He made a slashing motion with his hand. "Don't. Please." He couldn't stand it if she cried, if she pitied him. He turned toward the door, wanting nothing more than to be away from her, to figure out how and where all this had gone so wrong. "I think if you can go somewhere else for tonight, that'd be best. I'm going— I'm going to have to figure out what to do with you."

He heard her sharp inhale but couldn't focus on the fact he'd hurt her. He'd known things would end badly, hadn't he? How stupid to think he could take the risk. *Stupid.*

His words ricocheted in Maggie's head. She took a step forward, wanting to stop him, but knew she had to let him go. He closed the door behind him harder than necessary and she winced at the sharp sound. God. They'd gone from nearly making love to this. It was no less than she deserved but... Cody. Pain crashed over her in a sharp wave, chased by guilt. She'd brought this on herself. What she'd told Josh was true. There never seemed to be a good time. She'd intended to tell him, hoping that later the right moment would come. And, in fact, had been about to tell him tonight. If she'd managed to tell him before he'd found the pictures, would things have gone differently?

It didn't matter now.

She managed to pry her phone out of her pocket with shaking fingers and called Hannah, who answered on the second ring.

"Can I stay with you tonight?" Somehow she managed to get the words out through the tears clogging her throat.

"Of course." Concern laced Hannah's voice. "Maggie—"

She cut Hannah off. "Don't ask me," she whispered.

A slight pause. "Do you need any help?"

Maggie shut her eyes. "No. But thanks."

They disconnected, and Maggie stood very still in the room she loved, in the house with the two people she loved most in the world. None of it could ever be hers now. Unable to keep the tears from leaking out of her eyes, she threw some clothes in a bag and grabbed her toothbrush. She paused in front of the Christmas tree, her vision so obscured by tears it was nothing but a blur of colorful light. She unplugged it and left the room, closing the door softly behind her.

Cody stood in the hall.

She froze.

He blinked sleepily and frowned. "Where you goin'?"

She bit her lower lip. "To Hannah's," she said softly.

His frown deepened. "Why are you crying?"

Maggie touched her face. "Oh. I'm…just tired," she said and forced herself to smile at this little boy, her nephew, whom she loved so much. The tears burned fiercely, and she swiped at them. She couldn't let him worry. "You coming from the bathroom?"

Josh came up the stairs before Cody answered. His gaze locked on Maggie. She saw a flash of pain that was quickly replaced by ice. As angry as he was, he wasn't immune to the pain, either. It didn't make her feel any better. He moved between her and Cody. "Cody. Back in bed."

The little boy's eyes widened at the sharp tone, and his lower lip began to tremble. "But Daddy—"

Josh shook his head. "Bed, Code. Now." Eyes wide, Cody backed into his room. His gaze darted between them, and even through her tears, Maggie saw the worry on the little boy's face. She wanted to reassure him, but when she took a step toward him, Josh laid his hand on her arm, then snatched it back. "No." His voice was rough.

Then he turned his back on her and followed Cody into his room. The little boy's wails broke what was left of her heart.

Unable to stifle sobs of her own, Maggie ran down the stairs and fled the house.

Damn her. *Damn her.* Josh tried to comfort Cody but all he could do was blame Maggie for bringing this into their lives, for upsetting the careful order he'd established so thoroughly, for making him *feel*.

They'd been fine, just fine, and now they'd never be the same again. Thank God he hadn't had a chance to lay his heart on the line. He'd been on the verge of it.

"Why did you yell at Maggie?" Cody demanded.

He drew in a breath. "I didn't yell, Code. We had a disagreement and I—I asked her to leave. For a little bit. I think we are done with nannies." He was ready to move to a desert island until Cody was an adult. To hell with this relationship stuff. He was done forever.

"Why did she go?"

The plaintive note in Cody's voice was just one additional layer of guilt and pain. What could he say? *Maggie is your aunt? I fell in love with your mom's sister?* He could barely grasp this. How could he expect Cody to?

"She lied to me," he said finally. "That's not okay."

Cody's eyes rounded. "Oh. So she can come back when she says sorry?"

Josh almost laughed. "No. Some things even *sorry* can't fix, Code." She had apologized. Many times. Taken full responsibility for her actions, but he didn't know if it was enough. He didn't know if he could let it be enough.

"You won't let her be my mom," Cody said, and the accusation floored Josh. "You don't want me to have one! I asked Santa for a mom and you won't let me have one!"

Taken aback, Josh could only stare at his son. "Cody. No, that's not it at all. You don't need a mom, Code, we've done really well—"

"JT has a mom! All my friends do! But you won't let me have one." Hysterical, Cody's voice rose sharply. "I hate you! You made her leave!"

Whoa. "Cody. That's enough." Trying to wrap his mind around the anger, he reached out to touch his son. "It's not about not letting you have a mom. It's that I can't trust her." *Can't or won't?* He shoved the thought away.

Cody rolled over, his back to Josh, and burrowed down with Bear Bear. "Go away," he whimpered on a hiccup when Josh touched his shoulder.

Stung, Josh stood up and hesitated for a minute. Lost, he turned and left, Cody's sobs resonating in his heart.

Back in his room, he stepped over the pile of gifts and sat on the bed and stared at the TV. *It's a Wonderful Life* still played. Had it really taken less than an hour for his whole life to fall apart?

This is what he got for falling in love with sisters. *Sisters,* for God's sake. How the hell had Lucy not known about Maggie and vice versa? Why had Maggie thought deceiving him was the way to go? Was he so inflexible, like Lucy often said? Was that why she hadn't trusted him with the truth?

And why did it hurt so damn much?

Exhausted, thoughts circling and going nowhere, he lay back on the bed and drifted off into a fitful sleep.

When the on-call phone rang a little later, Josh realized he had a problem. Maggie was gone. He called his mother, who answered instantly.

"Josh! What's wrong? Is everyone okay?"

"Cody and I are fine," he assured her, then realized she'd catch his omission of Maggie.

"Maggie's not? What happened to her?"

That his mother would consider Maggie part of the family annoyed Josh in a way it shouldn't have. "She's not here. I asked her to leave. But now I'm called in." He stopped, unable to go on, exhaustion and emotion choking him.

"You asked her to leave? In the middle of the night? I thought—"

"You were wrong," he said roughly, and heard her sharp inhale.

"I see. I'll be over in a few."

She disconnected, and he wondered if she'd blame him as Cody had.

When she arrived, still in her pajamas, she looked at him, hard. He tried to give nothing away as he got his shoes on and shrugged into his jacket.

"What happened?" Her voice was quiet.

"Long story. I can't get into it right now." He took a breath. "Thanks for coming."

She nodded and made her way out of the kitchen as he left, trying to get switched into emergency mode.

He'd have to answer to her when he got home, and Cody, too. He paused a minute to scrub his hands over his face before he started the car and backed out. How everything had gone to hell so fast astounded him. But now, he had a patient who needed him.

Cody lay awake in his room. He heard Daddy leave and Gramma went in the bathroom after looking in his room, so he crept carefully out of bed. He needed to tell Santa to fix this. He wanted Maggie for his mom, and if Daddy wasn't going to listen, Santa had to know Maggie left. Maybe he could bring her back. It was dark still, so he found his Buzz Lightyear flashlight.

He went downstairs, Bear Bear under his arm. Santa would help him. He knew it.

Then he could have Maggie for his mama for Christmas and Daddy would smile again.

Santa would fix it.

Chapter Fifteen

Hannah asked no questions and for that Maggie was grateful. She led Maggie into the kitchen and offered wine and ice cream but Maggie politely refused both. She was afraid she couldn't keep anything down.

"I told him," she blurted, then buried her face in her hands. Hannah came over to give her a hug.

"Oh, honey. I'm sorry," she said as Maggie found she could no longer hold the tears and emotions at bay. Hannah eased her into a chair and left for a moment, returning to place a box of tissues next to her, then sat down and rubbed her back in little circles.

"Want to tell me what happened?" Hannah asked kindly.

"No. Yes." Maggie sighed. Then she filled in Hannah on the whole thing. How could everything fall apart in the space of an hour or so? It felt like a lifetime. Longer.

"Oh, Maggie." Hannah patted her hand. "Does he know you love him?"

Maggie shook her head. There was no point in denying her feelings, even though they no longer mattered. Until those last few moments before he'd found the pictures she hadn't thought he might feel the same or be willing to take a chance on them. She winced, the shock on his face playing in her memory again. She'd never forget his look for as long as she lived. Anger. Betrayal. Hurt.

He wouldn't want her to love him after this debacle.

"What are you going to do?"

Maggie sighed. "I don't know. I'm assuming he'll fire me. I guess I'll stay on until he can find a new nanny. Then I'll go…back downstate." She'd been about to say *home*. But that was no longer true. Holden's Crossing was home now.

How could she stay? How would that work, with Josh and Cody in the same town? The answer to that was simple. It wouldn't work.

Hannah frowned. "That sounds an awful lot like you are giving up, Mag."

She looked up, incredulous. "What else is there? I kept a pretty serious secret from him. It was a lie of omission. There's no way around that. If he trusted me, he doesn't now. What else is there to do?"

"You can fight," Hannah said softly. "Stay and prove you love him, that it was a mistake on your part but he can trust you. You meant well, Maggie. Help him see it."

Hope, that treacherous little flower, bloomed in her chest. Could she put herself back out there for Josh to reject again? What would it do to Cody? Was there a way to make it up to Josh?

Hannah touched her knee. "What are they worth to you? Sure, you didn't handle this the best way. But your intentions were good. Can you really walk away?"

Hannah was right. She needed to try, to at least make it right with Josh, even if in the end she did have to leave. She lifted her chin to meet Hannah's compassionate gaze. "No. I can't."

Now she needed to figure out how to make him see.

Josh's phone rang. With a frown, he noted his mother's number. He'd only been gone an hour. She wouldn't call unless there was a problem. "Mom? Is everything okay?"

"Cody's gone!"

Josh's heart stopped at his mother's hysterical words. He stood at the nurses' station, but the world had just gone wavy. The stark terror in her voice paralyzed him for a heartbeat.

"What do you mean, he's gone?" he asked, sure he must have heard wrong. Where would Cody go? It was dark and cold and snowing… Oh, God.

"I mean he's not in the house! His coat and boots are gone." Her voice pitched even further upward. "Josh—"

"I'm on my way. Did you call the police yet?" Panic bunched in his chest, an ice-cold chunk that made it hard to breathe. *Cody couldn't be gone.*

She hung up to call them and Josh simply looked at his colleague, unable to speak around the lump of fear in his throat. The other doc had heard enough of the conversation to wave him off, concern etched on his features. "Go, man. Call if we can do anything."

No one mentioned the bad weather or the slim chance of survival in it. He pushed the thought aside. He could not go there.

Agony swamped him. He couldn't lose his son. Cody had to be okay. *Had to be.*

He didn't really remember getting in his SUV. He also didn't notice much about the drive home, other than the falling snow. His phone was very quiet, no call to tell him Cody was fine, he'd just fallen asleep in his closet.

His coat and boots are missing.

Where would he go?

He whipped in the driveway, both horrified and gratified to see the police there already. Neighbors stood in the drive already, too, clearly preparing to search.

A sense of the surreal fell over Josh, as if he was living

someone else's life, as if he was going through the motions in a dream.

Only the cold was real.

One face stood out to him in the crowd.

Maggie.

He lurched toward her. God, how he needed her— then he stopped. She'd betrayed him. His mother, pale and clearly terrified, grabbed his arm as the officer, his childhood friend Brad Martin, came up to him.

"We're preparing to search," Brad said. He laid a hand on Josh's arm. "Can you think of where he'd go?"

Josh shook his head, frustration and fear welling. "No. I can't. I've been trying but—" But he could barely think beyond the loop in his head that kept saying *Cody's gone.*

"Did something happen to make him leave?"

"No—" Then it hit him. The thing with Maggie. Bile rose in his throat. "Yes. His nanny and I had a fight. I asked her to leave. He's very attached to her." Cody had been so upset. *So much for protecting him.*

Brad nodded. He'd no doubt heard the rumors about him and Maggie. "He may have gone looking for her."

Ellen came over to Maggie as Josh and the policeman talked. He looked awful, the harsh light turning his face haggard with worry and fear. Maggie's heart ached for him and for Cody, and she couldn't stop shaking. Where was he?

Ellen tugged her toward Josh. "He needs you now," she said, her voice brittle. "Be there."

For Cody, she'd do anything, so she followed the older woman over to Josh.

"Did Cody come looking for you?" The question was harsh. The accusation in his voice nearly leveled her. The policeman had already turned away to start the search parties.

"I don't know," she said honestly, worry for Cody nearly choking her. Could he have? He knew where Hannah lived. He hadn't come there.

Josh and Ellen stayed behind in case Cody came home but Maggie started out with the other searchers. As they fanned out, she prayed fervently that he was okay, that he was close, that he'd hear them. She clung to the heavy flashlight, looking under bushes and calling for him, her voice raw in her throat. The snow pelted her and froze the tears on her face.

The little boy's laughter rang in her head and the earnest look on his face when he'd talked to Santa— God, had it been yesterday? It seemed a lifetime ago.

Then she stopped. She'd never gotten a chance to tell Josh Cody's wish, for them to be a family. Shock rolled through her and she started to run. Had he gone back to the park, maybe hoping to catch Santa? He'd said he thought this Santa was real.

If she was right, there wasn't time to go back. She ran through the snow, chanting "please let him be okay" in time with her footfalls.

The band shell in the park loomed ahead. Behind her, headlights swept over the snow. She heard Josh's hoarse shout but didn't stop. Every single second counted. Her light bobbed in her hands as she flashed it over the open interior. It landed on— Was that a small form huddled on the floor of the band shell?

"Cody," she screamed as she got closer, barely noticing the sting of hot tears that streamed down her cold face. "Cody," she sobbed, sinking to her knees, not feeling the cold of the cement floor. "Please be okay. Please be okay," she whispered as the boy stirred and blinked at her.

"Maggie," he said, seeming surprised to see her.

Relief flooded her, flowed over her in a wave she couldn't break. She pulled him in close, even though she knew Josh was only steps behind her. "Hey, buddy. Lots of people are looking for you."

Cody burrowed in. "Sleepy," he murmured.

"Not a good time to sleep," she said, keeping her voice steady as Josh burst in and skidded to a stop in front of them.

"Cody," he whispered, relief and fear and joy all mixed in his voice. She saw the tears on his face, too. In that moment, she'd never loved him more and knew she'd never love another man again.

"Daddy," Cody whimpered. He lifted his arms. "I wanna go home."

Josh bent down and gathered Cody off Maggie's lap. He ran his hands and gaze over the little boy before tucking him against his chest. "We're going to go to the hospital first," he said. His gaze locked on Maggie's over Cody's head. "You knew."

She gave him a sad little smile as she got to her feet. "So did you."

Cody had gone looking for Santa. She had been sure of it. He'd thought this Santa was the real thing and had been confident he would come through.

Her stomach rolled. Cody wanted them to be a family badly enough he'd risked his life to try and find Santa. The thought made her stumble in the snow.

They trudged through the snow back to the SUV as quickly as possible. In his hurry, Josh had left it running, door open. Maggie hesitated.

"Get in," he said gruffly. "I'll give you a ride."

Not wanting to waste time arguing, for Cody's sake, she slid in and clasped her shaking hands tightly. They rode the few blocks back in silence. Ellen ran up to the SUV before Josh even had it in Park. He rolled the window down. "He's all right?" At Josh's nod, she pressed her hands to her mouth. "Oh, thank God."

"We're going to the E.R. to make sure," Josh said. "If we'd been much later—" The words trailed off, the ones left unsaid too hard to contemplate. Maggie saw the panic and fear mixed with relief on his face and her heart squeezed.

"I'll brief everyone," she said, opening the door. "Ellen, why don't you go with them? I'll finish this."

In the backseat, Cody gave a little cry. "No! I want Maggie."

Maggie froze, her hand on the door. Her gaze shot to Josh, whose jaw was set so tight she was afraid it would snap. "Cody. I, um—"

Ellen slapped her hand on the window frame. "You three go. I'll fill in Brad and meet you there. I'll only be a few minutes behind." She gave Cody a gentle smile. "Will that work, honey?"

He nodded, and Maggie closed her door. Josh rolled up the window and backed out of the driveway.

The ride to the hospital was tense. The roads weren't good and the combination of that, the stress from earlier in the evening and the fear and relief of Cody's rescue had Maggie very much on edge. Not to mention being in close proximity to Josh and unable to touch or comfort him caused an actual physical ache.

So she was relieved when they finally got to the hospital and she could move. Cody was whisked off, Josh at his side. He didn't even look back. Lost, she sank in a chair, grateful the waiting room was empty enough no one saw her blinking back tears.

She didn't know how long she'd sat there when Ellen

hurried in. She stopped at the nurses' desk, then came over to Maggie. "Why are you out here?"

Maggie closed the magazine she hadn't been reading. "I was just waiting."

Ellen frowned. "He left you out here?"

Maggie chewed her lip. What to say? It didn't appear Josh had said anything about what happened earlier. "It's all right. He was focused on Cody." As he should have been. Any problems they had paled in comparison to the fear of losing Cody.

Ellen looked at her for a long moment. "I see. I'm going to go check on my grandson. But then I'll be back."

Maggie stared at her retreating figure as she spoke to the nurse, then disappeared through the double door that led to the treatment area.

Ellen was back ten minutes later, looking grim. Maggie was on her feet, heart pounding, but Ellen shook her head. "Cody is fine," she said. "He's under lots of warm blankets, has the TV on. He'll no doubt be asleep soon." She blew out a breath as she sat down next to Maggie. "Josh, however, looks awful. Can you tell me what happened?"

"With Cody?" Though that wouldn't be much easier to explain about Cody's wish.

"No. With Josh." The older woman's gaze was steady. "Please."

Maggie agonized for a minute. It was her story to tell, since it was her fault. She took a deep breath and went for it. "I'm Cody's aunt. Lucy was my half sister."

Ellen didn't react, just stared at her. "I see."

Maggie wound her hands tightly in her lap. "I didn't tell Josh because— Well, for a lot of reasons that made sense at the time but things went much differently than I anticipated. If I could go back…" She trailed off because, well, she couldn't go back and fix it. No matter how much she wished it. It was silly to even think it.

"I'm not sure what to say," Ellen said finally. "You're right, you should have been up front at the beginning. I understand why he'd be angry. But the way he looks at you makes my heart happy. Is there anything else he doesn't know?"

Maggie met Ellen's serious gaze. "No. Nothing."

She gave a sharp nod. "I hope the two of you can work it out. You're wonderful with Cody and with my son, who's been so caught up in his misplaced guilt he's essentially cut himself off from the possibility of ever loving anyone. Now." She stood up. "Let's go see Cody. I know he wants to see you."

When Maggie and his mother came into Cody's room, Josh wanted to be annoyed. Or angry. Or anything but empty and lonely. The adrenaline from Cody's adventure had worn off and Josh was simply wiped, physically and emotionally.

Maggie went straight to Cody, who had dozed off about three minutes before they'd walked in. She laid a hand on his head, and Josh saw the tears in her eyes. God help him, he wanted to pull her on his lap and lose the awfulness of the night in her kiss.

But it wasn't possible now.

Since his mother was staring at him intently, he cleared his throat. The sound was sharp in the relative quiet of Cody's room. "He's fine. We got there just in time. No frostbite, though that probably was not too far away. He had his boots on the wrong feet, but they did the job. He'll be able to go home soon."

She gave a sharp little nod, and he could see those tears balancing on her lashes. Hell. If she cried, what would he do? He didn't dare touch her. He leaned over and picked up the box of tissues and held it out. She grabbed a few, murmured her thanks and sat down in the other empty chair.

His mother looked between the two of them, then raised her brow at him.

He still hadn't told her the story.

He put it off as long as he could, when they'd gotten Cody home and tucked in and Maggie returned to Hannah's. He wanted to tell her she could stay, but couldn't get the words out.

"Are you sure she should leave?" Ellen asked.

"Do you know who she is, Mom?" Josh tried to keep the bitterness out of his voice but failed. She'd brought nothing but trouble and he was done with it.

Except, he missed her terribly. And tonight, all he'd wanted was to have her by his side. To hold her and share the pain.

So much pain. It was crippling him.

"She's the woman who loves you," she said quietly.

Josh's head came up as the words arrowed into his heart. "No. She's the woman who betrayed me. She's Lucy's half sister, Mom." He could barely speak the words.

"I know. She told me tonight."

Josh stared her in disbelief. "She told you?"

She nodded. "I don't blame you for being angry. But do you want to throw away the possibility of a future with her?"

He leaned forward onto his knees and let his head fall forward. "Mom—"

Ellen laid her hand on his arm. "Josh. I know what I see. She loves you, loves Cody. I don't know why she didn't tell you about Lucy. But she brought you back to the world of the living again. For that I'm grateful."

Josh just sat there, processing his mother's words. "She lied, Mom."

Ellen nodded. "She should have been up front. I agree. But her feelings for you and Cody are genuine. Have you asked her why?"

"She didn't want to hurt us," he murmured.

"Did you listen to her? Really listen?" Ellen arched her brow.

Well, no. Not really. He hadn't been willing to listen. She nodded at his silence.

"I didn't think so. Before you write her and this relationship off, you need to talk to her and really listen to what she has to say. And you need to see once and for all that your relationship with Lucy was rough not because either of you were bad people, but because you were each with the wrong person." She leaned over and tapped him on the chin, forcing eye contact. "You made each other miserable. It was a two-way street. Love and marriage always is."

Her words struck a chord he would rather ignore. He needed the anger and the pain to keep the world at bay. It was the one thing he could count on to keep him and Cody safe—as long as he never let anyone in, there was no hope of him failing anyone.

Until today, when he'd failed Cody miserably and lost Maggie, too.

Ellen leaned over and kissed his cheek. "I'm going to get some sleep. It's been a hell of a night. You go lie down, too, honey." There was sympathy and knowing in her tired gaze.

Josh wished he could be as sure of the right thing as his mother was. Nothing was clear anymore—except he loved Maggie. Even now, knowing who she was.

And he didn't know how to stop.

* * *

The next morning, Maggie checked her phone—
again—and Hannah reached over to take it gently from her.

"This works both ways," she said softly, scrolling
through Maggie's contacts. "You can call to see how he's
doing." She pressed the phone back into her hand, Josh's
number on the screen.

Maggie shook her head. "I don't know—" she began,
as the phone rang. Josh's number came up on the screen.
She looked up at Hannah, who gave her a small smile and
a nod and slipped out of the room.

Hands shaking, Maggie answered the call. "How's
Cody?"

"He's fine," Josh assured her, his words and rich voice
filling her soul. She shut her eyes against the sting of tears.

"Oh, I'm so happy to hear that," she said. "Thank you
for letting me know."

A pause. Maggie held her breath.

"Can you come down?" he asked finally. "He wants
to see you."

Maggie's heart leaped. "Of course. When is a good
time?" Her words were a little unsteady and she hoped
he didn't notice.

"Now's good," he said.

"I'll be right down." She clicked off the phone and stood
up.

Hannah came back in the kitchen. "So?"

"Cody's fine," Maggie said. "He's asking for me so Josh
asked if I'd come down."

"That's a good sign," Hannah said.

Maggie shook her head. "I don't know. He'll do anything for Cody. It wouldn't surprise me if he doesn't talk
to me at all when I'm there."

Hannah frowned. "He's not that kind of guy. Besides, he loves you. He'll be there."

"Maybe he did once," Maggie murmured. "Not now."

"Love isn't something you just turn off when it doesn't work for you anymore. Not if it's real." Hannah's tone gentled. "From what I saw, it's real. Now go. Cody's waiting."

Maggie gave her a hug. "Thank you."

Hannah squeezed her back. "Good luck."

Maggie tugged on her parka and slipped out the door. The walk was short but both anticipation and worry weighed on her with every step. Cody was fine but was Josh? Would he say anything?

She walked up the front steps, unsure if she should just walk in. The door opened before she could knock, and Josh filled the doorway. Her heart simultaneously leaped and broke at the sight of him, pale and haggard, the shadows on his face indicating he hadn't slept much.

But, oh, how she loved him.

"Hi," she managed to say around the lump in her throat.

He nodded, stepped aside and she slipped past him into the foyer. Cody popped off the couch before she could get her coat off and he flew across the room and into her arms.

She sank to her knees and gathered him close, breathing in his sweet little-boy scent, tears burning her eyes. God, if it hadn't ended how it did— She shuddered. "Oh, Cody. You scared us."

"I know. I'm sorry." He burrowed into her, and she nearly fell over.

Warm hands landed on her shoulders, steadying her. Josh. Her body reacted instantly to his touch.

"Careful, Code," Josh cautioned. "You're going to knock her over. Let's go into the living room."

Cody held her hand as they walked in. Ellen came from the kitchen with a smile. "Hello, Maggie." Ellen held her son's gaze and a long look passed between them. "Josh, you're out of peanut butter. Cody and I are going to run to the store."

Cody peeled himself off Maggie with great reluctance. "Will you still be here?" he asked, and she nodded.

"I won't leave till you get back," she promised, and he sent his dad a sour look.

Josh nodded. "She'll be here."

"You can stay," Cody said earnestly. Then he threw his arms around her and held on tight. "I love you," he said, and those damn tears filled her eyes again. She inhaled the sweet scent of little boy.

"I love you, too, Code." *So much*. He slipped out of her arms and darted away.

Ellen came over and gave her a quick hug. "Don't let him get away with this," she murmured low in Maggie's ear and followed Cody out of the room before Maggie could respond that it wasn't up to her. After a minute of noise, the door closed behind Ellen and Cody.

Silence rang between her and Josh.

"Why didn't you tell me?" The anger in his voice had her blinking.

"About Cody and Santa? I didn't get the chance—"

"No." He shook his head as he spun around to face her. "Who you are."

Maggie sank down on the couch, feeling as if his words had pulled her legs out from under her. "I told you. I wanted to get to know Cody." What had been so simple at the time clearly hadn't been and had cost her everything.

He said nothing, just looked at her, his whiskey eyes shadowed. She took a deep breath. She had to make him understand. "I was lost, Josh. I'd lost my father, found out I had a sister—a sister!—then learned she'd died. I wanted to know Cody and I couldn't risk you telling me no."

Her words hung in the air. But they were the truth. No matter how it played out, she felt better for finally getting it all out in the open.

Josh sat down across from her, his arms draped on his elbows, head down. She clasped her hands so tight her fingers hurt but she welcomed the pain. Finally, he lifted his head and looked her in the eye. "Is there anything else you need to tell me?"

She held his gaze. "I'm sorry."

"Yeah. Me, too." His gaze shifted over her shoulder. "You can stay—for now." *Till I get a new nanny* was implied.

It was a start, a chance to prove herself. She'd take it. She gave a little nod. "That's fine. But you have to tell Cody something so he doesn't think I abandoned him. So he knows we can't be a family." She whispered the last few words, unable to fully voice them.

Pain flashed in Josh's eyes. "We'll tell him you have to go home. It's not a lie."

Her stomach curled as she stood up. In her heart, home was here, with Josh and Cody. But the consequences of her choice made that difficult. "No. It's not," she said simply. She moved toward the door. She'd get her things from Hannah's, come back and put on her game face.

For Cody's sake.

Chapter Sixteen

The past four days had been hell. Josh wanted nothing more than to fix everything, to put it all back the way it had been, but of course that wasn't the way it worked.

Maggie had let him know repeatedly how sorry she was, how she wished she'd been able to handle things another way. He wanted to forgive her, to let it go, to start over, but—

But. Well. How?

Now, on Christmas Eve, as he and Cody prepared for church, Maggie was conspicuously absent. She'd hugged Cody and told him she'd see him when he got back. So he'd go to church without her and after they'd go to his mother's for their traditional Christmas Eve. Hopefully she wouldn't mention Maggie. It was hard enough to have her in the house, where he could see her hips sway as she walked, hear her low laugh, smell her shampoo, but he couldn't touch her.

It was a physical ache, a hole in his life he couldn't close off or ignore.

He looked up as Maggie walked through the living room, small gifts in her hands. She turned quickly when he jingled his keys.

"Oh, sorry. I thought—" She trailed off, her cheeks red. She looked down at the presents.

"You thought I was gone," he said softly, and she straightened her shoulders.

"Yes." Their eyes met and the pain and betrayal and longing spun out between them. He felt as if his heart would be pulled right out of chest with the force of it.

"Maggie." Her name was almost a plea. For what? This couldn't be fixed. No matter how he wished it, they couldn't go forward.

"Josh," she whispered, tears shimmering in her big blue eyes. "Go. You'll be late."

He spun and left before he pulled her into his arms and told her the truth he couldn't get past—he loved her.

Somehow, he got through the church service. The lighting candles part required concentration and his mother kept frowning at him, but he emerged from the church in one piece.

Cody skipped at his side, his boots making deep prints in the snow. "Can we go to Gramma's now?"

"Yep, as soon as she comes out," he said, managing a smile for his excited little boy. Christmas was purely for Cody and he'd do his damnedest to make it a good one.

Well, other than making his fondest wish come true.

"Will Maggie be there?"

The hopeful words may as well have been stones. "No. She's at home, remember?"

Cody's frown was visible in the light of the streetlamp. "You're mad at her."

Was he? Josh didn't even know anymore. He was trying to be, but mostly he was just numb. But he wasn't going to go down this road with Cody, especially not on Christmas Eve. "She needed to finish some stuff so she stayed home." He managed another smile. "It'll be just you and me. And Gramma."

Cody frowned. Josh held his breath and hoped his son would drop it. This was not the place to get into why Maggie wasn't here. He couldn't put off Cody forever. When and how did he explain Maggie was really his aunt? Or why she had to leave?

Thankfully, his mother popped out of the church right then, and Cody seemed to forget about their conversation. They all rode together back to her house. Cody kept up a steady stream of chatter, Josh only partially listening, since his mother kept the ball rolling. "And Santa said it's a season for mary-cles."

That snapped him out of his thoughts and he hit the brakes a little harder than he should have. His mom frowned at him. Before he could speak, she did. "He's right, Cody."

Josh felt sick. "Mom." The warning should have been clear. But she ignored him.

"Anything is possible on Christmas Eve," she said serenely. "Isn't that true, Josh?"

He said nothing, not wanting to acknowledge what she was really saying. "How long, Josh?" she asked in a low voice when they got in her driveway and Cody hopped out. "How long are you going to hide behind Lucy?"

Trav had said the same thing to him a few weeks ago. "Mom. I'm not hiding."

"Oh, posh," she snapped. "You damn well are. Shut yourself all the way down because you decided you are responsible for Lucy's death. For how crappy your marriage was," she said fiercely. "And now you'd deny yourself and Cody the chance at love? With a woman who's your match in every possible way?"

Her words pinged inside him. "It's not that simple."

"Sure it is. Don't be a coward, Joshua." And she shoved

open her door, climbed out and slammed it hard enough to rock the SUV.

He sat there. Opening himself—and Cody—to more destruction was exactly what he wanted to avoid. These past few days had taught him that. It wasn't cowardly to be careful and protective. It was—

Wussy.

No, damn it. It was smart. He shook off the thoughts as the Christmas-tree lights in the house went on. He could see Cody looking out the window. He quickly got out of the SUV and strode up to the house. They'd do this. And tomorrow, when Cody's miracle didn't come through, he'd pick up the pieces and try to put them back together. So they could get back to normal.

You mean empty. Lonely. With a huge hole where Maggie should be. He ignored the unhelpful little voice. They'd find some kind of normal, one way or another.

He sat through the present opening, trying to focus and be engaged for his son. Cody was very excited about his gifts from Gramma. Josh frowned when Cody put an awkwardly wrapped package on Ellen's lap.

"Wait, Code, is that supposed to be here?" he asked, leaning forward to check the tag. Cody nodded.

"I made it. And wrapped it. Maggie helped," he said proudly, and Josh felt the air rush out of his lungs.

"You did a lovely job wrapping," Ellen told him with a smile as Cody nestled in next to her. She carefully unwrapped it while Cody wiggled at her side. Josh saw her eyes fill with tears as she lifted out what looked like a concrete round.

"Oh, Cody. It's beautiful." She turned it so Josh could see. Cody's handprint was in the middle and Maggie had carved his name and the date on it. He could imagine them working together in the garage while he was at work, her dark head bent next to Cody's lighter one, laughter in their sparkling blue eyes.

Maggie loved Cody, and he loved her. He couldn't deny it. Now he'd gone and taken her away from him. Like he'd done with Cody's mom.

"You did a great job, Code," he said, his voice a little rough.

Cody beamed. "I put all the rocks in," he said, patting the shiny stones. "And I had to wash my hands a lot 'cause this stuff was supermessy."

Ellen kissed the top of his head. "I love it. Thank you. For now it will stay inside and in the spring you can help me find a special place for it outside, okay?"

He nodded and slid off the couch to play with the truck set Ellen had given him.

"Josh, you want a cup of coffee?" It was phrased as a question, but he knew better.

"Sure, that'd be great. Thanks." He followed her into the kitchen and took a seat at the breakfast bar as she took down two mugs. She set them on the counter, poured and wordlessly set the milk in front of him. He focused on stirring the white liquid into the coffee, not wanting to look at his mother and what he'd see on her face. More accusation, no doubt.

Finally, she spoke. "You never answered my question."

Josh's head snapped up. "I'm not hiding." But somehow, he couldn't muster the heat behind the words he always had in the past. He was also too exhausted to try. Trying to pretend everything was okay, that he wasn't torn to shreds emotionally took everything he had.

Ellen folded her arms and just looked at him.

Josh shut his eyes, wishing the tactic that worked so well for Cody at age four when he wanted to disappear still worked at age thirty-four. "Mom. Please."

"Josh." Her voice was intense and he forced himself to meet her eyes. "Don't do this."

He let out a sharp bark of bitter laughter. "Do what?"

"Avoid the real issue here."

"You mean other than Maggie lying to me?"

Ellen's gaze never flinched. "Yes."

He scrubbed his hand over his face. Maybe if he just played along she'd leave him alone. "Okay, Mom. I'll bite. What am I avoiding?"

"Lucy." Her words were firm. "Don't," she added sharply when he leaned forward to stand up. "You've avoided this for far too long and look what's happened. You've let the best thing that's happened to you slip away."

Stunned, Josh could only stare at her. "Excuse me? Maggie lied to me."

His mother shook her head. "You're letting Lucy run your life. You are trying so hard to be everything to Cody, to make up for her being gone. It was not your fault she died, Josh. You did not take her from Cody."

The familiar guilt flared. She was wrong. Everything he'd done for the past four years had been built on that. If he tried hard enough to give up everything she could no longer have, then maybe he'd make up for not loving her.

"It takes two," Ellen said quietly. "There were two of you in your marriage. I've said it before. You weren't right for each other, anyone could see that. How many more times do you need to hear it before you believe it? Lucy was a lovely young lady and a wonderful mom to Cody. You both tried to do right by him. But she wasn't right for you."

"I was a terrible husband," he said with a raw laugh, ignoring the ring of truth in her words. "I was never there for her. I couldn't give her what she needed."

Ellen slapped her palms on the counter and the coffee

cups sloshed. "Was she a terrible wife? Did she give you what you needed? Was she there for you?" When he realized he couldn't answer, she went on, her gaze lasered in on his. "Why do you insist on hanging on to this?"

Because I can't fail someone again. But he had, hadn't he? He'd failed Cody. He opened his mouth, then shut it again. She nodded. "If you were truly torn up by grief I could see it," she said softly. "If she'd been your soul mate. But this is guilt. Far more than you need. You did not put her in that car. You did not make her drive it. You did not cause her to crash. She hit the patch of black ice. It was an *accident*—an awful, tragic accident."

He felt everything collapsing around him and gripped the mug of rapidly cooling coffee. "Mom. We fought, said awful things. She was so angry…." He trailed off, remembering the hatred on Lucy's beautiful face. His last memory of his wife was grounded in anger and that wasn't fair. He remembered the accusations from his in-laws and shook his head.

But Ellen beat him to it. "No. You did not cause it. Horrible things are said in anger, honey. No matter what Hugh and Jeanine said, you did not cause Lucy's death. They know you didn't. The sooner you forgive yourself for being angry, for not being the husband you wanted to be, the sooner you can let her go and move on."

Forgive himself. Was it truly possible? Josh looked at her. "I don't know, Mom." To let it all go—

"You can still honor her memory," she said patiently. "It's not about forgetting her or even whitewashing the memories. But hiding behind all the bad stuff is not the way to do it."

Something clicked in Josh then. Of course she was right. And despite his best intentions, he had in no way honored

Lucy or helped Cody. Instead, he'd let his guilt complex color everything. "Oh, God."

Ellen sat back, her gaze steady and understanding. "Don't start over with the recriminations, honey. Forgive yourself—forgive Lucy. And forgive Maggie, too."

Josh's gaze snapped to Ellen's. "That's a lot of forgiveness."

She gave him a small smile. "You're up to the task. You love Maggie. She loves you and Cody. Work through this with her."

Work through it. He contemplated the cooling mug of coffee in front of him. She'd lied.

But she thought she was protecting you. He knew in his heart she'd believed what she'd done was for the best. While he didn't agree with her method, he understood what she'd been trying to do. How hard it must have been to learn about Lucy—and realize she'd never had a chance to meet her sister. He also wasn't sure how he'd have reacted if she'd come to him as Cody's aunt, asking to meet her nephew.

He also knew his mother was right. He'd hid behind Lucy's death so he could protect Cody…and himself. What if he failed again? What if he did give Maggie another chance and they couldn't make it work?

Cody would get hurt. He'd protect his son from everything bad if he could.

But that wasn't how life worked.

Cutting Lucy out of their lives and losing Maggie were two of the worst things he could do—for both him and Cody.

He had to go to Maggie. He pushed back his chair and his gaze slid to Cody, still playing with his new truck in front of the Christmas tree. "Mom—"

She cut him off. "Go." She gave him a watery smile.

"Whatever happens with Maggie, I'm proud of you for finally seeing the truth. Cody and I will hang out for a little bit. We'll eat cookies and play with trucks."

He dropped a kiss on her head, getting a whiff of the sweet scent he'd associated with his mom his whole life. He threw on his coat and jogged to his SUV, barely noticing the bite in the winter air. He fervently hoped he wasn't too late—he hadn't screwed things up so badly he couldn't fix it.

It was time for Cody's miracle.

Maggie settled in her sanctuary upstairs. She figured she had some time before Josh and Cody came home. She plugged in her tree, since it was the thing to do on Christmas Eve. There was no joy in the evening for her, though. Not anymore.

Santa wouldn't be coming through for Cody. The knowledge absolutely killed her. He'd wanted this badly enough he'd run away, trying to find Santa to tell him the situation was critical.

Worse, she'd be leaving soon after Christmas. Not the ending she wanted, but it really couldn't have gone any other way. Not once her secret was out.

She'd started packing. She'd carefully stashed everything in her closet, because she didn't want Cody to see and get even more upset.

But there was no alternative. She couldn't stay here. She'd look for an apartment after Christmas. Close enough she could help out until he hired a new nanny, but far enough away she could breathe. Maybe even start to heal.

The whole idea left her feeling hollow and exhausted. She'd lost both Josh and Cody, the two people she loved more than anything. How, exactly, did she heal from that? If she was lucky, Josh would allow her to stay in Cody's life.

When the door banged downstairs far earlier than she expected, she jumped up and hurried out in the hall to see Josh plowing up the stairs, still in his boots and wool dress coat. Her heart leaped into her throat. She raced toward him, panic closing like a vise around her throat.

"Josh! What's wrong?" *Please don't let Cody be gone again.*

Josh stopped on the top step so she was nearly eye level with him. She could smell the damp wool of his snowy coat, the aftershave he used, the scent that was so uniquely Josh it nearly took her to her knees right there.

Their gazes locked. In his she saw fear and sorrow and longing—and something more. She put her hand to her throat. "Josh?" His name was barely more than a croak.

His hand curled around the banister. "Cody is fine."

Relief hit her, and she sagged a bit. She couldn't take it if something bad happened to him again. "Thank God."

"It's me."

She held herself very still. "You." Her nerves went on alert. "O-kay."

He took her chin in his hand and her knees trembled. His hand was cold but still felt good—too good—against her skin. She couldn't take too much of this. "I'm so sorry, Maggie."

She blinked. "Why?" What on earth did he have to be sorry about?

He pulled his hand away and she felt the loss of contact keenly. "We need to talk."

"Now?" Her heart kicked up. "Where's Cody?"

"Now," he said softly, and she saw the softness in his eyes. "Cody is with my mother. I need to talk to you alone."

"Ah." She turned and walked into her room, amazed she could even stand, and he followed, shrugging out of his coat as he went. "Well. What did you want to talk about?"

Her voice was almost calm, which was amazing considering the crazy rioting butterflies in her belly.

She wrapped her arms around herself and perched on the edge of a chair, afraid to breathe, afraid she couldn't handle what he wanted to say. Could her heart break any more?

She didn't want to find out.

He stood very still, his gaze on the Christmas tree that provided the only light in the room besides the fire. Finally, he took a long inhale and turned in her direction. "I've been using Lucy as a shield." His voice was raw. "I've been hiding behind my dead wife. Your sister," he added softly. She sucked in a breath. "And so have you."

Maggie drew back and shook her head slightly. "No." Of course she hadn't.

He moved closer and took her hands in his. Her hands shook slightly. She met his gaze, uncertain of what she'd see there. "You came here and didn't tell me who you were out of fear we'd reject you. I've done it to keep from making another mistake." He shut his eyes for a second, then opened them. "We made a mistake, Lucy and I. But it was on both of us. I've tried to be both parents, to protect Cody. As if somehow I could make it up to him, you know?" At her teary nod, he went on, his voice low. "I didn't make her get in that car. She left on her own. I'll never stop feeling awful," he added, "but it was an accident. I've hauled around a lot of guilt. While I'm not going to say some of it wasn't deserved, I didn't handle it like I should have. That was made crystal clear when Cody ran away the other day. I can't—I can't stop bad things from happening."

"Oh, Josh." More than anything, she wanted to reach out and pull him to her. Instead, she tightened her grip on his cold hands. He squeezed back and let go.

He stood up. "Let me finish. I can't stop bad things from

happening but I also can't stop living. That's pretty much what I was doing, as my mother pointed out to me multiple times over the past few years. I thought I was honoring Lucy by not having a life outside Cody. If she couldn't, I wouldn't. But really, it wasn't about her. It was about me." He came over and kneeled in front of her and laid one hand on each of her knees. His face was inches from hers and, unable to stop herself, she laid one hand on his cheek. He caught it in his and looked at her earnestly. "But then you came in our lives and in spite of everything, we both went and fell in love with you."

It took her a moment. Then a lightness bubbled up from deep inside. "What are you saying, Josh?" She was almost afraid to ask, for fear she'd heard wrong.

"I love you, Maggie." He gripped her hands tightly, and in his whiskey gaze she saw everything she'd been afraid to hope for. "I need you in my life. We need you," he amended with a rueful laugh. "My boy is clearly smarter than his old man. He had it figured out long before I did."

She laughed through her tears—these were of joy, not pain, finally—and leaned forward into his arms. "I love you, too," she said, tipping her face to his. "And Cody, too. Maybe he gets his smarts from his mother's side of the family?"

Josh chuckled, and his warm breath feathered across her lips. "I bet that's it," he murmured before he claimed her mouth with a gentle kiss. A delicious heat curled around them, and the rightness of it all began to fill the hole created when she'd thought she'd lost him forever.

He pulled away and rested his forehead on hers. "No more secrets?"

"None," she agreed, joy flooding her. "But—when do we tell Cody who I am?"

"How about tonight?" Josh suggested. "Actually...after

this." He leaned in and kissed her thoroughly till her head spun. Then he gave her a wicked grin. "That's just the beginning."

She smiled back. "I certainly hope so."

"Let's go tell Cody." He took her hand and together they hurried out to his SUV. The trip to his mother's took a bit longer than normal, since he kept pulling over to kiss her, but Maggie wasn't complaining.

Ellen met them at the door. "Did you—" She stopped as Maggie stepped from behind Josh. She laid her hands on her heart and Maggie saw the hope in her eyes. "Oh. Does this mean—?"

Josh wrapped his arm around Maggie, and she snuggled into his side. "Yes. It means I came to my senses." He dropped a kiss on Maggie's head, and she smiled up at him, then at Ellen.

"Merry Christmas, you two," Ellen said and pulled Maggie in for a hug. "Welcome to the family."

The words sent a little shiver down Maggie's spine. She hugged Ellen back. "Thank you. I'm so happy it worked out."

Ellen patted her shoulder. "'Tis the season, my dear. Now. You'd better tell Cody."

"Good idea. Cody?" Josh called.

The little boy popped out of the living room, his gaze darting from his dad to Maggie to their joined hands. His eyes widened. "Daddy! Will Maggie be my mom?"

Josh half turned to her. "I hope so," he said and the intensity of his gaze warmed her heart. He turned back to his son. "Cody—Maggie's already your aunt. She and your mom were sisters who didn't know each other."

Maggie held her breath but Cody just nodded. "You can be my mom, too?"

Her heart overflowed at the hope and joy on his face.

"Yes. I can. I'd love to." He had no idea how much this meant, how very much she loved him and his father.

"Whoa, Cody, this is my part here." Josh laughed and gave his son a quick one-armed hug. Cody beamed up at both of them. Josh turned his attention back to Maggie, and her breath simply stopped at the look in his eyes. "Maggie. I love you—"

"We love you," Cody interrupted. "Don't forget that, Daddy!"

"We love you," Josh amended with a grin, then dropped to one knee right there in his mother's foyer. Maggie's heart swelled so much she thought she might float away. Josh's face was serious as he took her hand in his. "Shoot. I don't have a ring yet. But Maggie Thelan, will you marry me?"

"Us," Cody corrected, and Maggie laughed even as the tears—of joy, this time—began to fall.

"Yes," she said, looking deep into Josh's whiskey-brown eyes. "Yes, I'll marry you. Both of you," she added as Josh started to rise and pull her into his arms. Cody flung himself between them, squeezing their waists as tight as he could.

"Santa did it!" he crowed. "I knew he would!"

With a laugh, she met Josh's gaze over Cody's head, saw the love in his gaze and knew she'd truly come home.

Epilogue

Cody met Maggie at the door after her doctor's appointment. "Mom! Lucy's crying again!"

Maggie paused for just a moment to hug her adopted son and kiss the top of his head. "Thanks, honey. I'll get her. She's probably hungry."

She continued up the stairs only to run into her husband holding their baby daughter. The six-week-old fussed and whimpered, and Josh smiled at her. "Someone wants her mama," he said as he handed the baby off, managing to brush her breast in the process. He wiggled his eyebrows. "Oops."

Maggie leaned in and stole a kiss from her sexy husband. "According to the doctor, I'm all clear for all normal activities," she said, and when his gaze brightened, she laughed. "After I've nursed this little sweetie. Oh, and Cody goes to bed. And they actually are asleep at the same time." She wouldn't trade a minute of the upheaval the addition of the baby had created in their lives. She'd found out she was pregnant almost immediately after their January wedding. Now, in October, she found it hard to believe one year ago she'd taken the job as Cody's nanny, just hoping for the chance to know him. Now, she was his mom—and both she and Josh kept Lucy's memory alive in their lives.

Josh followed her into baby Lucy's room—Josh's old bedroom—where she settled in the glider rocker and put the baby to her breast. His smile was slightly naughty. "We'll make it work."

She met his gaze over Lucy's downy head, saw the heat and the love and once again felt a little shiver that he was hers. "I know."

"I do have a surprise." He leaned on the doorjamb.

"Really? What's that?"

"Gramma Jeanine and Grandpa Hugh want to take Cody to dinner." He looked hopefully at her. "Maybe Lucy will take a little nap?"

Maggie laughed and gestured him toward her. When Josh bent down and braced his hand on the arm of the glider she gave him a kiss. "That can be arranged." She hoped.

He dropped a kiss on their baby's head. "Awesome. Did you hear that, sweet pea? We're going to make you a little sister or brother."

"Ha! I'm not quite ready for that yet," Maggie said with a laugh as he left, whistling. She rested her hand on Lucy's soft little head. "But soon," she promised. "Very soon."

After all, with Josh and their love, anything was possible.

* * * * *

A sneaky peek at next month…

Cherish™

ROMANCE TO MELT THE HEART EVERY TIME

My wish list for next month's titles…

In stores from 15th November 2013:

❑ Snowflakes and Silver Linings – Cara Colter

& Snowed in with the Billionaire – Caroline Anderson

❑ A Cold Creek Noel & A Cold Creek Christmas
Surprise – RaeAnne Thayne

In stores from 6th December 2013:

❑ Second Chance with Her Soldier – Barbara Hannay

& The Maverick's Christmas Baby – Victoria Pade

❑ Christmas at the Castle – Marion Lennox

& Holiday Royale – Christine Rimmer

Available at WHSmith, Tesco, Asda, Eason, Amazon and Apple

Just can't wait?

1113/23

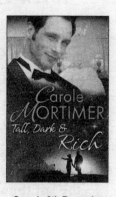

Wrap up warm this winter with Sarah Morgan...

Sleigh Bells in the Snow

Kayla Green loves business and hates Christmas.

So when Jackson O'Neil invites her to Snow Crystal Resort to discuss their business proposal… the last thing she's expecting is to stay for Christmas dinner. As the snowflakes continue to fall, will the woman who doesn't believe in the magic of Christmas finally fall under its spell…?

4th October

www.millsandboon.co.uk/sarahmorgan

1013/MB435

Join the Mills & Boon Book Club

Subscribe to **Cherish**™ today for 3, 6 or 12 months and you could **save over £40!**

We'll also treat you to these fabulous extras:

- 🌹 **FREE L'Occitane gift set worth £10**
- 🌹 **FREE home delivery**
- 🌹 **Rewards scheme, exclusive offers…and much more!**

Subscribe now and save over £40
www.millsandboon.co.uk/subscribeme